BOUND BY HER BLOOD

MARA LEIGH

Half Dome Press

Cover design: Covers by Juan
ISBN: 978-1-989318-04-1 Print Edition

FOREWORD

Dear Reader,

This is a quick note for **sensitive readers**. If you'd rather avoid all spoilers, please turn to the next chapter.

But, if you have possible triggers please read this content warning.

BOUND BY HER BLOOD is an ultimately uplifting story, but it starts in a dark place. The heroine suffered abuse in her childhood and is being held captive at the start of this story. She's now a vampire, so she can heal, but there are some descriptions of sexual abuse in the opening scenes and some description of the torture and abuse she's survived in the past.

In addition, later in the book, it's revealed that one of her heroes also has a very traumatic past that includes sexual situations.

If these story elements might be triggering for you, or if you aren't up for very steamy scenes with graphic language, then this book might not be for you.

CHAPTER ONE

Selina

Today, I am going to die.

It's not the first time I've thought King Xavier would kill me. Not to mention the countless days and nights before my capture when I thought my end was near, but no matter how many times I've been close to death, it doesn't get easier—or more welcome.

And King Xavier has lost patience.

Each time I fail to complete the ceremony, the powerful vampire king grows more angry, his punishments more brutal—and on the last new moon he swore my next attempt would be my last.

No way will I survive another wedding.

"Come, Selina. Today's your big day." Jordina, one of Xavier's mates, gestures for me to step into the warm bath where she and Alexander are waist deep, their bodies' glistening like sculptures of a Greek god and goddess, and nothing short of magnificent.

Held captive at King Xavier's court for over a year, I'm

still not used to the nudity and sexual openness here. My hand trembles as I unbelt my red silk robe.

"Don't look so frightened." Alexander smiles warmly, his deep brown eyes transmitting comfort. "You'll complete the ceremony this time. I'm sure of it, and then you'll be part of our family."

Although the king prefers females, Alexander is also one of Xavier's mates, and if I complete today's wedding ceremony, I'll be mate number nineteen. I'd rather die.

I drop my robe to the tiled floor, and the red silk spreads like fresh blood across the gleaming marble tiles, leaving my body exposed to everyone in the baths.

A loud exhale comes from a dark corner of the room.

I lift my gaze.

Pike.

My hands fly up to cover my body, and my belly tightens with fear. Pike's the most vicious of Xavier's King's Guard, and his immense size is a fraction of what makes this particular vampire so utterly menacing.

His huge body shifts. Thick arms barely reach across a bare chest that's marred by a jagged scar, slashing red and stretching from one shoulder to slip under the waistband of the worn leather pants that hang from his hips.

Pike's eyes, amber and piercing, penetrate the darkness. Shivers trace through me as if his gaze is visceral, scraping over my body and peering into my soul—adding salt to my many wounds.

Eager for cover, I accept Alexander's hand and descend into the warm, rose-scented water.

"Isn't she beautiful?" Alexander says to Jordina as if I'm not there. "Such a perfect age when she turned." Lifting my hand over my head, Alexander twirls me around like we're on a dance floor, not a small pool.

"Gorgeous," Jordina whispers near my ear.

Using soapy fleece mittens, she strokes up and down my arms, over my back and shoulders, and then slips the mitts under the water and over my butt.

Relax, I tell myself. *Allow yourself to enjoy the pleasant moments of this day*, but it's not easy, I know what's coming.

Once Jordina finishes with my back, Alexander guides me onto the partially submerged lounging bed in the center of the bathing pool.

"Head back." Jordina holds up my lavender hair as I relax my neck into the cradle that seems custom designed for me, even though I'm sure all of King Xavier's mates use this bath.

The female vampire pours warm water over my head, and I inhale the citrus scent of the shampoo as she washes my hair, giving my scalp an intoxicating massage. Weak from months of starvation and torture, my body yields to the warm water and the vampires' gentle touches.

As Jordina washes my hair, Alexander dons the soaped mitts and washes my throat, my belly, my breasts. His caress is firm but tender and sensual, and if I keep my eyes closed, I can imagine his are the hands of a lover, even though imaginary lovers are the only kind I've had. Not that I haven't been fucked.

Since I've been captive at court, I've been abused too many times to count, and although I've been blindfolded during most of those assaults, I feel sure the worst of them have come from Pike.

I shudder, knowing he's here in the room, his eyes on my naked body. My insides squeeze as if those muscles could protect me from his punishing member.

"What's wrong?" Alexander pauses, his hands on my breasts, and I open my eyes to find genuine concern in his.

"You know what's wrong," I say flatly.

"Selina." He strokes his hand down the middle of my torso to stop low on my belly, circling there. "Resisting will only bring you more pain. Give our king, give *us*, a chance. Is Xavier a demanding lover? Yes, he is. But I love him, and if you let yourself, you will love him, too." He smiles at Jordina and she nods, a blush rising on her cheeks.

"And you'll love being *our* mate," she whispers in my ear, then kisses the lobe.

Alexander backs through the water toward my legs, and his erection juts through the water, bouncing near his abs. Is his arousal for me, or because he's been talking about his mate?

It doesn't matter. And he's wrong. Even if I get through the ceremony—doubtful—I will never, ever, love King Xavier.

As Jordina massages my temples, Alexander lifts one of my legs and washes the length of it, spending extra time on my upper thigh. Then his mitten slides over my sex, stroking the plush fabric back and forth, way beyond what seems necessary to bathe me.

"Oh, Selina." His voice is throaty and deep. "I know our king will have the privilege of taking you first, but I cannot wait to be inside you."

Alexander acts like he doesn't know what's been happening to me in the dungeons. Perhaps he doesn't. If he knew, how could he love King Xavier? How could any of his mates love the king if they knew what happens in his dungeon? Did any of them refuse the king like me?

As Alexander strokes the mitt over my sex, a wave of pleasure courses through me, in spite of the situation. In the less than two years since I transitioned into a vampire, my sex drive has multiplied exponentially.

When I was human, I totally avoided sex—any contact with men—but since I became a vampire I've found myself unable to control my body's reactions to stimulation—even when it's not welcome.

My supercharged libido is my least favorite thing about being a vampire—and that includes having to drink blood and missing out on sunshine.

But I can't lie. Being bathed by these two kind and beautiful vampires is sensual, even if my arousal makes me angry. How can I be turned on after all that has happened, and given what's *about* to happen?

I want my first *real* love-making experience, my first time that's *my choice*, to be with someone I love, but at this moment, I have to admit that the idea of sex with Alexander—or Jordina—is appealing, and being part of the king's harem would at least free me from being tortured by his Guard.

Can I go through with this? Marry the vampire king?

Luxuriating under Alexander and Jordina's skilled hands, I can almost imagine my life as Xavier's mate, but then I remember the vampire king himself.

My entire body tightens.

"Poor Selina." Alexander kisses the multitude of round scars on my inner thighs, gifts from my stepfather.

Cigar burns were how my stepfather showed his displeasure when I showed mine at how he forced his penis inside me. He started when I was eight, less than a year after Mom married the monster.

I quickly learned how to check my mind out of my body whenever he'd visit me at night, but my compliance didn't please him either, and the monster found new ways to torture me besides penetration.

When I finally escaped the house at fourteen, I believed

I was free, that I'd already suffered the worst things that could ever happen to me—to anyone.

Then I met King Xavier.

Selina

After my bath, Alexander and Jordina apply my makeup and style my hair. I won't get through the ceremony, which leaves me two choices: escape or death.

"Do you like your hair this way, Selina?" Alexander asks, and I open my eyes for a moment. He's curled my hair into dozens of tiny ringlets that he's looping and pinning at varying lengths using tiny diamond-encrusted clasps that sparkle against my pale purple hair.

I nod, noting the heavy black eyeliner Jordina applied, the metallic silver eye shadow, and, of course, the blood red lipstick. Objectively, I know I look good.

I hate it.

Beauty's a symbol of my captivity. My desirability is the trait that led to this misery.

If only I'd disfigured myself before I transitioned, but at twenty-two I'd been hopeful, no idea my physical self would be forever frozen in place.

And my lavender hair color, now permanent, came the very day I was turned. I was so happy when I splurged on that hair dye—a treat to myself for landing my dream job in graphic design.

After years of living on the streets and then in roach- and predator-infested rooming houses, I was on my way. Starting a job I knew I'd love. Soon, I'd be able to afford a real apartment. One where I didn't need to share the halls with roaches or registered sex offenders.

But the very night I dyed my hair, I was attacked by a vampire who nearly drained me and left me for dead in an alley. Somehow I turned all on my own—which is supposedly impossible.

Clearly it's not.

So many things I thought I knew about vampires aren't true. But one thing is true—they, we—thrive best in groups.

Surviving on the streets, a lone female vampire without a syndicate or kingdom for protection, wasn't easy. Still, I managed it for three months until the fateful night I met Santos and was tricked by his kindness.

Santos brought me here to Xavier's court, and presented me to the king like a cat dumping a dead mouse on the kitchen floor for its human.

Seconds later, Xavier plunged his fangs into my neck. He fed from me until I was so weak I could barely stand, then the king declared I was his. Since that night, my life's been so full of torment and agony it makes my abusive childhood, my teenaged years on the street, seem idyllic.

One way or another, today will end all that. I only wish it didn't have to end in my death.

Makeup and hair done, I stand still, and Jordina adjusts my wedding gown, this one even more elaborate than the previous twelve. In several hues of red, narrow panels of silk and crushed velvet intertwine as they drape my body, highlighting my shape and leaving my breasts mostly exposed, as well as my throat.

The embroidery thread is twenty-four-carat gold, as are the beads and tiny sequins hand-sewn along the neckline and slits, which reach from the floor all the way to my waist—front and back.

Jordina slips me into a thong. A triangle of red silk encrusted with tiny diamonds advertises my sex below the apex of the gown's slit. The string reaching back from there is fashioned from a series of large black pearls.

Jordina's fingers part my labia to position them, then she tugs up on the garment from behind, adjusting the length of the string until the orbs press hard into my sex, creating stimulation each time I move—or breathe.

I vow to minimize both at all costs.

Alexander takes a gold hoop from a tray and opens it. Without warning, he pierces my right nipple. I gasp, and my involuntary movement digs the pearls into my sex.

Alexander fastens the ring and slides it back and forth through the hole, then, using his finger, he wipes blood from my breast and pulls it between his lips, his eyes closing in ecstasy.

"Selina tastes delicious," he says to Jordina. "I can see why Xavier wants her so badly."

Alexander pinches my other nipple, making it hard, and then pierces that one, too, but this time I'm better prepared for the pain.

Jordina doesn't bother with her finger and takes my nipple, hoop and all, between her lips. She sucks, circling my nipple with her tongue several times.

"Oh, my," she says as she licks a few stray drops of blood from my breast. "You *are* going to be a very popular member of our family."

She crouches and her hand slides under the gown to circle my ass, then she tugs up on the beads from behind. I open my eyes to find her smiling, her expression swimming with desire.

Her hand lightly traces forward through my folds, then up the front of my gown as she straightens. "Selina. Please let love fill your heart today. Don't resist him this time. Please."

"Yes." Alexander puts his lips on my neck and licks the skin over my pulsing vein. "If you let him, Xavier will worship you."

"And so will the rest of us," Jordina adds. "Even if Xavier sometimes gets rough, we'll *always* make you feel good."

"So good." Alexander pushes his hand between my legs and fondles the pearls.

I squeeze my eyes shut, trying to fight my body's reaction. These two vampires are sexy AF, and the way they're touching me—tenderly, almost reverently, compared to the abuse in my past—drives my desire up to eleven.

Can I actually do this? Marry King Xavier? Join this family?

Already powerful, with each new mate King Xavier grows more so. And as one of his mates I'll have protection for eternity. No one outside our family will dare touch me again.

Tired, hungry, tortured, I admit the idea is tempting.

"She ready?" A deep male voice invades the space.

Pike strides in, his heavy boots echoing around the dressing room.

My heart rate quadruples. Why him? Of all of Xavier's Guard, why do I have to be walked down the aisle by the most despicable, most cruel, most menacing vampire I've ever encountered?

"Just a couple of finishing touches." Alexander dips a brush in a pot of red powder, then carefully decorates my nipples, already fully healed from the piercing. If there's one advantage to being a vampire, it's quick healing, although that one thing doesn't make up for everything else vampiric. Not even close. I so miss being human.

I inhale the distinct coppery scent of the powder he's using, intoxicated by the unmistakable odor of dried human blood. Starved for so long, I wish I could bend to lick it off.

Jordina clips the end of a gold chain to my thong, securing it tight against my clit. Where is the other end of it going?

"All ready," she says.

With horror, I realize the other end of the chain has a leather handle—and Jordina hands it to Pike.

Below bushy dark hair that falls to his shoulders, the massive vampire's eyes narrow as he ogles my body, shaking his head slowly and licking his lips. No doubt the beast is thinking of all of the filthy and painful things he wants to do to me. If I marry Xavier he won't get another chance.

His head turns, and I gasp. Caught at the right angle, Pike is handsome, in a brutish, ultra-masculine way. Even though his right cheek is scarred in an angry red mess, no doubt badly burned before he turned, I can imagine how he might once have looked. Standing before me, Pike's impossibly broad chest expands and contracts, each breath lifting pecs as solid and pocked as ancient shields.

Empathy rushes my heart. Are Pike's scars, the pain he suffered, what created the cruelty inside him?

No. I have scars and they didn't make me cruel. More likely Pike's wounds came from a woman trying to defend herself from him. I shake off my momentary softness.

Should I try harder with the ceremony this time?

I shudder at memories of my past wedding days. The very first time I walked down the aisle followed a period of relatively conventional courting—conventional for Xavier—and he made genuine efforts to win me over to his affections.

But that first time I refused to speak my lines during the ceremony.

My defiance led to a month of nightly assaults, like he thought he could use his body to force love into mine. But during wedding attempts number two, and three, and four, I again refused to recite the words.

After that, Xavier's distinction between punishment and coercion blurred, and his techniques turned more brutal. He moved me from the small room next to his into the dungeon where I'd be under the "care" of his Guard. His Guard made Xavier seem gentle.

The seventh marriage attempt followed a night after I was penetrated endlessly by Xavier's female Guard members equipped with huge dildos—the worst bachelorette party ever.

That time I gave in. I spoke all the ceremony's words. All I knew was I wanted the torture to end. That day I did resolve to marry him. I thought all it would take was saying the words, but it didn't work.

Since then, I've been defiant, and I've suffered for it.

If I try today, on lucky marriage number thirteen, if I try to *mean* the words as I say them, try to *feel* the words in my heart, then maybe this time will be different. Maybe today I'll end up one of Xavier's mates—married for all eternity to a vampire I'll never love.

As horrible as that sounds, it doesn't seem as bad as being dragged back to the dungeon by Pike—if Xavier even bothers with the dungeon this time. More likely he'll make me suffer some horrible humiliation and death in front of the entire court.

CHAPTER TWO

Selina

Four other members of Xavier's Guard stand outside the dressing room, all uniformed the same—bare chested with leather pants—and all carrying sharp wooden stakes. Two of them walk ahead of Pike, and two take places behind me, their stakes no doubt angled toward the left side of my back.

As we walk down the dimly lit corridor, my knees tremble and I grow short of breath. I haven't fed from a human vein since I failed my fourth marriage ceremony. Since I've been housed in the dungeon, I've had only thimble-sized sips of stale blood—barely enough to keep me alive.

I try to keep my eyes on the flagstone tiles, rather than Pike, but find myself mesmerized by the huge mounds of his ass cheeks, like steel pressing out against the worn leather, and by the undulating muscles of his back, fully engaged in keeping his huge mass upright.

Keeping the chain slack between us, Pike walks slowly

enough for me to keep up, and twice the guards leading our procession have to stop to let us catch up.

But that small kindness ends when we enter the Great Hall.

The instant we're in sight of his king, Pike tugs hard on the handle, pulling it forward and up, pinching the tender flesh of my vulva and nearly pulling me off my feet as he jerks me into the room.

Dozens of crystal chandeliers hang over what looks like hundreds of vampires, all dressed in black and white.

Red, the preferred color at court, is reserved today for the bride and groom.

Flanking us, the guards continue up the aisle, our hideous wedding party walking more quickly now. Pike tugs on the chain, urging me to keep up—or possibly just to be cruel—and by the time we near the altar, my vulva's burning, and my clit is so sensitive I fear I might come.

The guards in front part to stand at either side of the large marble platform. Pike tugs me forward until I'm mere feet away from the king, and then he holds the chain taut, tugging aggressively against my sex.

Cruelly handsome, King Xavier's jet black hair is smoothed back from a strong-jawed face that frames lush lips, and his bright green eyes are accented by heavy but well-groomed brows. His red leather suit perfectly fits his strong, lean body and molds over the protruding bulge at his crotch.

All I can see is ugly.

He smiles and pure evil emanates from every pore in his body.

Try this time, I coax myself. *If you don't marry him, he'll kill you.*

"I like the leash," he says to Pike. "Well done."

Pike tugs up on it—hard—and I gasp.

Xavier's eyes open wider. "Did that thing get her good and ready?"

"See for yourself, Your Majesty," Pike answers.

"No, you do the honors. Please." Xavier shoots me a look, full of malice.

"Your Majesty. I couldn't. She's yours." Pike's voice is hoarse and deep.

"That wasn't a suggestion," Xavier says. "Unless you'd like to exchange your living quarters for a stall in the dungeon."

Pike turns toward me, looking down, avoiding my eyes. Not that I want to see the cruelty I feel sure I'd see there.

"Spread your legs for my loyal guard," Xavier demands.

Before I can move, the guards behind me kick my legs apart so abruptly I nearly fall.

Pike presses his long, thick middle finger against his equally huge index one and shows them to Xavier, who nods.

Pike sucks in a long, ragged breath, then he slides his fingers between my legs, drawing back and forth a few times over the beads. I fight against my body's arousal as my breath expels in a thready burst.

"Do you like that?" Xavier asks me.

I shake my head.

He chuckles. "Put them inside her," Xavier says. "I want to make sure she's prepared." He wants no such thing. He only wants to show his dominance—over me, over Pike, over everyone in the room.

Pike's chest heaves sharply in reaction to the king's command, and then he forces one finger inside of me.

I squeeze my eyes shut, trying to ignore my body's traitorous acceptance of the intrusion.

"Let me see," Xavier commands.

Pike withdraws, then holds up his index finger.

Xavier studies it for a moment and then licks my juices off its tip. "Not deep enough." He steps back. "All the way in. At least three fingers." He nods to the guards. "Secure her legs."

Pike's breath catches again as the guards take hold of my ankles and spread my legs even wider, holding them there.

Pike holds his pinky down with his thumb, making a rod with his three middle fingers and showing them to Xavier. The king nods his approval. Then, with his other hand on my shoulder for leverage, Pike plunges his digits inside me—hard and fast.

I cry out. Even though I'm so wet, the sudden thick intrusion is painful.

Another effect of my rapid healing is that my channel has remained as tight and sensitive as it was when I ran away from home at fourteen.

Yes, my stepfather violated my body many times before that, but as I learned here at court, that monster was endowed with a pencil dick. Since my transition, each time I've been penetrated by anything thicker than a thumb, it's like my first time.

Pike pulls out his hand and shows his damp fingers to Xavier, who nods, smiling.

"Selina, my love," Xavier says. "Look at me."

I reluctantly raise my gaze to meet his, and he licks my juice off Pike's fingers, wet all the way to the bottom knuckle. Xavier sucks the large vampire's digits into his mouth as if tasting the most succulent dish. Pike looks angry, probably wishing he could have used his whole fist.

"Very nice." Xavier steps toward me.

I almost fall back. The guards are still holding my ankles.

"Let her go," he tells them and then he cups my face in his hands.

"My beautiful Selina." He kisses my forehead and looks into my eyes. "I cannot wait for you to be my mate, to share myself with you daily in wedded bliss."

I shudder.

"Darling." The look in his eyes turns almost compassionate. "You don't yet understand how magnificent it is to fuck and feed from your true mate, the power we'll *both* derive from our pairing." He presses a light kiss against my mouth, then slides his lips close to my ear and whispers, "Yield to me, Selina. Love me and I'll protect you forever."

He straightens, leaving no evidence of his tender plea on his face as he gestures for the priest.

The priest leads me onto the marble platform and wraps a sheer white silk scarf around my neck, letting the ends drape down my back. Then he does the same to his king.

At each of the past ceremonies, my white scarf ended up soaked in my blood, or torn from my body, or both. Xavier's neck has yet to be pierced. If I pass today, will I be capable of plunging my fangs into his neck as he fucks me to complete the final step of the ceremony?

My intense hunger for blood rises at the thought.

I can sense the power of the king's blood as it pumps through his veins, and I fight a battle inside myself. In spite of my revulsion, my body hungers for Xavier—in more ways than one—and my survival instinct wants me to comply, to do all I can to make this work.

Listening to his blood gush inside him, I force down my

hatred as desire floods through me. I want him to feed me, to fuck me. Fuck me here and now in front of everyone.

I shake my head quickly. What is happening to my mind?

I do want to live. Do I want it badly enough to go through with this marriage?

"My children," says the priest. "Do you come here today of your own volition, without coercion or threat?"

I glance at the wooden-spike-wielding guards, still aiming their weapons at me. "Yes, we have," Xavier and I respond together.

Hearing our voices in unison, my unwelcome feelings for Xavier grow. I certainly feel lust—both blood and sexual —but love?

"And is your love true?" the priest asks.

"It is," we both answer.

The vampires at court exhale a collective sigh, and the crystal chandeliers seem to brighten, filling the cavernous space with warmth and light.

"Do you promise to love and protect each other for all of eternity?"

"We do."

"We do, too," Xavier's other mates say in unison as they gather closer, and I can sense the blood pumping through all eighteen of them. I feel their desire for the king, for me, for each other. I concentrate on those positive feelings. They all love him, can I?

"Do you promise to worship each other, your bodies, your eternal souls?"

"We do," I respond to the priest. I've said all these words before, but today's the first time I've said them earnestly, desperately wanting them to be true. It's the only way to survive.

"Then it is time." The priest gestures.

Two small vampire boys approach. They look ten years old, but I learned from Jordina that one of them is over two hundred, frozen in time, just like I'll forever look twenty-two.

Each of the boys holds a small golden cup, and the priest places a large golden bowl, ornately carved with scenes of mating couples, on the floor between us.

Xavier steps toward me, and the hunger in his eyes is so powerful I can taste it, *feel* it in my bloodstream and between my legs. At this moment I believe that Xavier loves me, in spite of his cruelty. And in this moment I want him, too. I want him to feed from me, to fuck me, to call me his mate. Fueled by my weakness and thirst, my fangs tingle, wanting out.

Xavier sweeps me against him, pushes my head to the side and plunges his sharp fangs through the silk scarf and into my vein.

I moan. It feels like the force of a thousand horses are pulling blood from my veins, pulling every cell in my body up and off the ground, and the rush is almost as good as the first time I fed from a human.

But the feeding is over almost as quickly as it started, and it leaves me even weaker.

Xavier releases me, and I stumble back.

"Kneel, my child," the priest says.

I kneel on the cold marble.

Lifting the scarf, the priest holds my head to the side as one of the boys collects the blood that drips from my open vein, catching every drop in his cup, until the puncture wounds close.

King Xavier kneels opposite me.

One of his mates, Sylvia I believe, approaches and

kneels beside him. They look deeply into each other's eyes and it's impossible not to see their mutual desire, plus what looks like genuine love between them. Will I feel that, too? Can I?

Xavier holds out his wrist to her, and she slashes it open with her fangs, drinking a few long gulps before holding his wrist out for the other altar boy to collect the royal blood in his cup. She kisses Xavier with her blood-drenched lips.

"Thank you," the priest says to Sylvia.

Xavier breaks their kiss, licking the last of his blood from her chin, and then she stands, backing into the shadows as the altar boys each hand their cups of blood to the priest.

It's the moment of truth.

If our love is real, if the words we spoke were true, then our blood when combined in the ceremonial bowl will combust.

My heart thuds in my chest, unsure of which outcome I want as the priest speaks incantations and raises the bowls high above his head. Slowly, he tips them.

The blood seems to flow in slow motion, one drop at a time descending toward the larger vessel below. The thick liquid strikes the bowl's surface on both sides and drains toward the bottom, the streams sliding slowly toward each other to determine my fate.

The first drops touch. Xavier gasps. Then our bloodlines completely intertwine and turn into... a small pool of blood.

"Liar!" he shouts. "You don't love me at all, you conniving little whore!"

One of the guards lifts me roughly to my feet and immediately all four of the wooden stakes are pointed directly at my heart—two points in front, two in the back, one so firmly against me that blood trails down my exposed skin at the front of the gown.

"Shall I grant you an easy death, Selina?" Xavier glares at me, hatred completely replacing the flash of love I saw earlier. "Should I command my men to penetrate your heart with those stakes right now?"

Eyes narrowing, he shakes his head. "What a waste that would be. It only takes one stake to kill you. Perhaps the other three should penetrate you first—in all of the places I've fucked you."

"One down your throat." He pushes his finger forcefully between my lips, then walks behind me. "One in your cunt." He bends me forward and forces his fingers inside me. "But first, I think, a sharp stake in your asshole."

I hear gasps and cheers from the crowd, then something sharp scratches my anus. No. He won't. Even Xavier wouldn't do that.

I'd heal. Even this starved of blood, I would heal, but it wouldn't make the injury less painful or humiliating.

"Let me!" Pike's heavy boots shake the platform, and I close my eyes bracing for the pain. "Let me take care of her, Your Majesty. I will be sure that she suffers."

Xavier laughs. "Very well! Take her out of my sight, Pike. Use her as you wish and then kill her."

CHAPTER THREE

Selina

Pike carries me draped over his shoulder. As we press through the room, the crowd tears the gown and thong from my body. They pull the diamond clips from my hair, the rings from my nipples, and fangs pierce my skin everywhere they can reach.

Unwilling to die without a fight, I struggle against Pike's hold, but he's too strong. And the other vampires are persistent with their groping fingers and fangs.

My very undignified exit from the Great Hall proves that Xavier's promise is real; there's no chance he's going to go back on his threat to kill me this time. There's no chance he'll attempt wedding number fourteen.

If he held out any hope we'd be married, he'd never allow this.

In spite of what he's let happen to me in the dungeons, King Xavier would never marry a vampire who's been used like this by his court.

Grunting, Pike starts to run, pushing the others off my

body and out of his way. Clearly he wants to keep the pleasure of torturing me to himself, and by the time we reach the dungeon, I'm nearly passed out from the combination of fear and pain and hunger.

He drapes me forward over an all too familiar padded bench, its leather stained with blood. My upper body falls over the far side of the angled bench, leaving me bent with my ass up, and I'm too weak to resist.

I hear the clank of the shackles as he closes them around my ankles and wrists, but I'm so delirious, I can't even sense the metal bindings' bite.

Pike secures leather straps around my waist to hold me in place, then standing in front of me, he places my chin in a ring to support my head, leaving my neck exposed and my face angled downward.

A strip of leather inside the ring covers my eyes, and soon it will be tightened around the back of my head to prevent both sight and movement. I've been prepared in this setup many times before, left like this for weeks at a time, but today I've got nothing to lose. I'll bite off any cock that gets near my mouth.

But to my astonishment, instead of a cock I sense Pike's wrist in front of my captive face, his vein exposed, within fang-striking distance.

"Drink," he says.

"What kind of sick fuck are you?" My voice is hoarse and weak. "You want to make me stronger so your abuse can last longer?"

My hunger's so overpowering, my need for blood so heightened, even Pike's blood smells enticing. More than enticing. With his wrist so close, his blood smells like a combination of the most delicious things I've ever tasted: rare steak, chocolate, a fresh peach on a hot day.

My fangs release and I lick my lips, unable to control myself as my entire body yearns to have Pike's blood in my mouth, in my body.

But I don't strike.

He presses his wrist against my mouth. I hold my lips closed.

I already caved in to one evil vampire today, said things I didn't mean, convinced myself that I wanted things I didn't. I won't let it happen again.

I do need blood to survive, but refuse to take his, even though Pike's scent makes me want him more than I've wanted anything—ever. If I'm going to die, I'll die with an ounce of dignity.

As I squeeze my lips tight, my fangs dig in to my own flesh and my mouth fills with my blood. I gulp it down, wishing it could help build my strength. But with my blood coming out of one place in my body and going into another, I'll only grow temporarily weaker as I drain my blood supply faster than my body reabsorbs it.

The struggle to keep my lips closed is so hard it hurts.

I not only smell Pike's blood, I can hear it. I've heard the heavy rush of blood before, but this is different. Pike's blood sings to me in a voice so alluring, so overtly sexual and beautiful it overtakes my mind, my body. But that only proves how far gone I am. I'm so near death, I'm hallucinating.

The door creaks and a set of footsteps signals that another guard's in the room.

"You done fucking her ass with that spike?" a male voice asks, and I hear the sound of a zipper. "I want a turn before the blood dries."

"Come near her," Pike tells him, "and I'll rip your dick off."

"Okay, okay." The guard chuckles along with the sound of steel scraping on stone. He's removed one of the weapons from the wall. "I won't use my cock, then. This will work nicely."

My chest heaves in fear, remembering the barbed spears, the studded metal dildos and other objects on the walls of the dungeon.

I long to die quickly. Die now before these monsters do whatever they have planned.

After my last few marriage ceremonies, Xavier's guards were cruel, but now that their king is officially done with me I'm fair game. For anything...

Fear overtakes every part of my body. Shaking, my eyes covered, I can barely hear or smell or think. I can barely breathe.

"Get out!" Pike yells. "You heard the king. She's mine. I am the one who gets to fuck her. I'm the one who gets to kill her. Me. Don't come back. Spread the word. Anyone sets one step on the stairs to the dungeon, anyone sets one foot in these halls without my permission gets staked."

"Okay, okay. Be greedy." The metal object clangs against the floor.

The hinges creak, then the heavy door slams.

I am again alone with Pike.

With my toes barely touching the ground and my ankles spread wide and shackled, my legs tremble. Pike presses his wrist against my mouth.

"Drink." He strokes my hair. "You're going to need your strength. Please."

At that last word, I almost yield. But even more than I want his blood, I want to yell at him, to scream in defiance.

But I can't risk it.

If I part my lips, even a millimeter, I won't be able to

resist his vein. Pike wants me strong so his torture will last longer and as much as I want to live, I will not satisfy his vicious desires.

But my own vampiric urges may be stronger than my will, stronger than my mind. During the ceremony, those urges tricked me into thinking I could love King Xavier. A monster.

I don't love him. I could never. Just like I could never take a taste of the savage beast who's tempting me now.

Pike finally withdraws his wrist.

I gasp and then lick my lips, ravenous for blood. Pike's blood.

Even blindfolded, I know he's moved several feet away. I can still smell him, hear his blood, imagine its taste.

I've been hungry before, but never thirsted like this.

From behind me, Pike's hands land on my shoulders, and I brace, ready for penetration and pain, but instead, he strokes my throat, licks my barely pulsing vein. His hands trail softly over my naked body.

"Rest," he says as he strokes me. "No one will dare come down here until I say. And know this. If you leave here, I will find you. No matter how far you run, I will find you. And yes, some day I am going to fuck you. I'm going to fuck you again and again and again. I'm going to fuck you until neither of us can stand, until neither of us can breathe. But not today. When I fuck you, you'll want it. And you're going to want it even more than you want my blood right now."

Want Pike? He's delusional.

Yes, he saw me nearly cave to Xavier, but the idea that I'd ever have sex with this beast—willingly? Not a chance.

As I lie trapped on the bench, Pike licks and kisses me, running his firm tongue and lips over every inch of my exposed skin—my back, my ass, my inner thighs.

And I hate my body for how it responds as his mouth caresses me in ways that are at once comforting and arousing. My mind is repulsed, but my body isn't. Instead, wetness pools between my legs and my skin heats, and I find it hard to keep my hips still against the bench.

His lips leave my skin, and I hear the unmistakable crunch of fangs as they plunge into flesh, but I feel no pain. Instead I feel the warm drip of blood on my shoulder blades.

Pike paints my back with his blood, his hands massaging, no doubt marking me as a threat to the other guards. He's determined to be my sole inflictor of torture, the one to kill me.

His blood absorbs into my skin, and the feeling is powerful, energizing—arousing.

My hips circle, and the strategically placed ridge on the bench finds my clit.

I still myself. *More* aroused is the last thing I want.

Pike breathes heavily behind me. I hear and feel his labored breath even as I continue to smell and taste the promising song of his blood.

Just when I can barely stand it, just when I'm about to cry out for his vein against my mouth, to beg for his dick to impale me, he leaves.

Pike leaves me alone in the dark with only my fear and the anticipation of more pain that I know will most certainly end in death.

~

Selina

After Pike leaves me in darkness, I yield to the lure of the bench's ridge and grind my clit on it until I come.

My orgasm explodes, pulling every part of me inward as if my body's imploding into my pounding core.

When my breathing returns to normal, I realize the sensation of drawing inward wasn't just my climax-induced imagination. Parts of my body actually *did* move.

Parts I know can't move while I'm restrained on this bench.

But my legs definitely drew closer together.

I release the wooden handles from my tight grip and I discover my wrists aren't clamped either.

I lift my head and the leather strap behind it easily yields.

Weak and blood starved, I can barely see in the darkness, but realize I'm not tied down except at the waist. I reach back and fumble to unbuckle the leather strap constraining my torso.

The second the buckle yields, my body slips off the bench. My legs refuse to support me, and I land crumpled on the cold stone floor.

Pike must have thought me so weak he didn't even bother to tie me down. He only restrained me enough so I wouldn't fall.

Or maybe this is his sick game? Maybe he wants a hunt before his kill?

Even fully fed, my strength would be no match for Pike's, or any of the king's guards. Even with the dungeon weapons on the wall, I can't fight Pike and win.

But doing nothing also means death.

Even if it plays directly into his plan, I have to try to escape.

Struggling onto my hands and knees, I smell blood. Human blood.

Following my senses, I creep forward on hands and knees until I find a small bowl of the nourishing red liquid.

I lap like a kitten until I find the strength to lift the bowl and drain it. I must have found the vessel they use to provide me with teaspoons of blood at a time. As my belly fills and the blood absorbs into my bloodstream, my night vision returns.

Weakly, I stand.

Pressing my ear against the wooden door, I hear nothing in the hall outside.

I tug on the handle and wince as the heavy door creaks on its hinges. After a quick check, I slip into the hallway. I've never been down here on my own, and never noticed much of this corridor beyond the flagstone floor.

The walls are also stone and they're damp, like I'm far underground. Without lighting, it's hard to make out many details, but I see a piece of cloth hanging from a hook on the wall. I tiptoe forward to retrieve it, hoping it's something I can use to cover up my blood-smeared, naked body.

When I reached the cloth, I discover a trench coat and quickly put it on, belting it tightly around me, and then I look up and down the hall, trying to choose a direction.

The direction I came from leads toward the Great Hall, and even though the failed wedding ended some time ago, the hall's likely still filled with vampires. Vampires out to torture me for rejecting their king.

Choosing the lesser of two evils, I head forward into the unknown.

The corridor turns several times, and I pass many closed doors much like the one I came out of. I try not to think of the possible prisoners behind those doors. I'm not even sure I can save myself.

I reach a dead end, and my heart sinks as I press my forehead against the cold damp wall there.

A slight breeze tickles my skin.

My palms roam the damp wall, trying to find a crack, a handle, anything. I scrape my nails and fingers over the surface, not caring if they become raw—I'll heal if I live—and I finally discover a tiny stone jutting out from the rest.

I push it. Nothing happens.

Gripping it tightly between my scraped thumb and index finger, I tug on the stone. Part of the wall slides open.

I quickly slip through the opening and run, hearing the door close behind me. Not that the closed door will help much. I assume Pike knows about this passage, and once he discovers I'm gone, he'll come after me. It's not like a closed door will slow him down.

The passage is narrow, but the ceiling is at least seven feet high and I guess—I hope—that it's a way out of the palace, used by King Xavier's Guard when they go out to hunt or recruit—like the night Santos found me.

Like switchbacks up a mountain, the uphill passage slopes and turns many times until it ends at a metal door. Without hesitation, I open the door, then quickly slam it shut.

Daylight.

My face, hands, shins and feet sizzle, all my exposed skin fries in the sun. I should have taken another second to consider the burning star's angle, so I could estimate when it might be safe to try again.

But the direct sunlight is too much to bear for more than an instant. On my second attempt, I don't get an indication of time, either. Instead, I use my sunburn as a timer.

Each time I'm healed enough to open the door, I try again, then again, determined to keep opening the door until either Pike finds me, I'm burned to a crisp, or the sun has set, whichever comes first.

Living in the palace these past fourteen months, I've lost all concept of time, of night or day. I figured the wedding was scheduled at night, but had no idea. Contrary to legend, vampires have no preference for night or day, as long as we can stay away from the sun. No sunlight ever penetrates Xavier's fortress, except where and when he wants it to.

During my punishments, I often suffered sunlight torture, exposed to short scalding bursts of light that ravaged my skin. Xavier would reopen the light tunnels each time I nearly healed, and then when I was burned, he would kiss me and soothe me and try to convince me to love him.

I lived through that torture and worse. I can live through this, too.

Bracing against the pain of my burns, I huddle in the darkness by the door, listening for signs of Pike and wishing I'd had more than one tiny bowl of human blood to sustain me. Each time I open the door, it takes longer to heal, and I won't last much longer.

Xavier liked me to be yearning for blood at each ceremony, and clearly that part worked. He made me want him today; he made me want Pike.

I press my healing cheek against the soothing cool metal of the door. After I escape the palace, then what?

Before I was captured, I'd only been a vampire for three months, and I spent all of it moving from place to place, seeking out the basements of abandoned buildings for shelter and surviving on the alcohol-diluted blood of drunks staggering down alleyways before dawn.

As a lone vampire, especially a lone female, I was endlessly hunted by the syndicate recruiters—and the human police.

Humans discovered vampires were real when I was a little girl. Since then, all police carry stakes.

Vampires have no rights. For us, there's no innocent before proven guilty. We don't get judges. There are no juries of our peers. Police have orders to kill vampires on sight.

That's why the syndicates and kingdoms exist—for protection. Strength in numbers. At least, that's what Santos argued to lure me to Xavier's court in the first place. But if life at court is what protection looks like, I'd rather live in danger.

Feeling strong enough, I try the door for the fifth time. Fresh air brushes my still stinging face and relief floods through me as I step into an alley, between rows of tall buildings, and look up at the twilight-hued sky.

I smell humans, many humans, even though none are in sight.

No idea where I am, I let the door close, then realize I can't go back through it, even if I had the desire—or death wish. Closed, the door blends so well into the wall I can't even see where it was.

I cautiously walk down the alley, looking up at the buildings, searching for landmarks. I assume it's still Toronto, but Santos blindfolded and drugged me before taking me to the palace, so I can't be certain.

I reach an intersection, and the CN Tower peeks between two buildings.

I know where I am. But it's been over a year. Do any of

my daytime hiding spots still exist? I have until dawn to find out.

But first, I need to feed. Feeding is risky this soon after dark, but I head toward the Entertainment District, hoping to catch someone on the way home from after-work drinks.

Luckily it's spring, so my trench coat doesn't look out of place, and I slink through the vibrant city streets, tugging the coat around me, hoping it covers Pike's blood, and lets me pass as a human.

CHAPTER FOUR

Selina

Four hours later I'm beyond famished. The tiny bowl of blood I found in the dungeon wasn't nearly enough to sustain me, especially after months of starvation combined with healing from today's multiple sunburns.

Without feeding, I will never survive until dawn. And this time of year, dawn will come soon.

My ideal meal ticket should be someone alone, preferably a straight male I can lure somewhere private, but the only men I've spotted have been in groups, or with women, and none looked like a promising meal.

Not an *easy* meal, anyway. And tonight I need easy. I need the McDonalds of blood feasts—fast and effortless and out of a readily disposable container.

Not that I plan to kill my dinner container. Not if I can help it.

Guilt floods inside me. Not since the very first time I fed have I killed a human. But tonight, like that first night, I'm so hungry and out of control, I'm not positive I can stop feeding once I start.

Giving up on the Entertainment District, I wander west toward the Junction, close to the tracks where the streets are quieter, a mixture of old factories, houses, and a few funky coffee shops and bars.

I'm stronger and faster than a human, but slow for a vampire, and I feel at risk in my weakened condition, not to mention my *naked* condition. The only thing I'm wearing under this trench coat is Pike's blood.

I shudder. Even worse than the risk of human detection, Pike is surely hunting me now. Can he track his scent? Is that why he marked me with his blood? I wish I knew more about my own kind.

A light rain starts to fall as I stand in an alley near one of the only factories that's not yet converted to condos. I let it wash over my face, almost tempted to take off the trench and let the rain wash off all the evidence of Pike.

A man turns the corner from a street parallel to the alley, and hope rises in my chest. Alone, dressed in a suit and walking with a slight stagger, he's likely been out drinking since work, and with any luck I'll be able to lure him deeper into the alley.

My target meal hails a cab and disappears. *Crap*.

Dizzy with hunger, I head down the alley, hoping I might find a safe place to rest. Or if I get even more desperate, a rat.

"Hey there." A man steps out from the shadows.

I jump back. Even though I'm a vampire, I haven't lost the instincts of a human woman. I know the math. Strange man + alley = danger.

Ha! These days I'm the danger.

"You lost?" he asks.

I shake my head as I size him up and glance around to make sure he's alone, that we aren't being observed. Have I finally found dinner?

"Whatcha got on under that trench?" Hooking his finger under the knot at my waist, he tugs me forward and looks at me with the most revolting kind of hunger. The hunger of a man who wants sex and nothing else—and I'm not talking *nice* sex either. His is the hunger of a man who thrives on overpowering anyone weaker.

My instincts scream *run*, but I remind myself that I'm the one who can overpower this human.

"Come." He tips his head down the alley. "It's more private down here."

I narrow my eyes. Does he think it's that easy? Would any woman be stupid enough to follow him into the alley?

Even *I* don't want to follow him, and I want to eat him.

Grabbing my arm, he yanks me forward. I fall to my knees on the damp asphalt. I'm weaker than I realized.

"Get up." Roughly grabbing me around the waist, he lifts me to my feet.

His arm pins mine against my sides as he yanks me aggressively along the alley. Before I can react, my foot lands in a rain-filled pothole. I stumble.

"Fucking drunk," he says with obvious disgust.

To keep me moving, he pulls me even harder against his side, and my bare feet scrape along the broken asphalt as I fight to find my footing.

"I'm not paying for this," he growls.

"Paying?"

"To fuck you."

I wrench myself out of his grip. "What makes you think I'd fuck you?" I no longer even want to drink his blood.

"Bitch." He grabs my hair, yanks hard and turns me, pushing me face first into the damp brick wall.

My face hits before my hands, and the impact stuns me, giving him the advantage—for an instant. He holds my cheek so hard against the wall I'd have a brick patterned bruise on my face for weeks if I were human.

I feel a tug at my waist and my coat's belt drops to the ground. He flashes a knife near my face—one he obviously just used to cut off my belt—and then uses his body weight and other arm to pin me.

"One peep out of you and you're dead," he growls in my ear as he gropes the front of the coat, presumably looking for buttons that aren't there. He rips the garment off my body, nearly tearing one of my shoulders from its socket.

I no longer care if I drink this guy dry. In fact, I can't wait to kill him.

"What the fuck? You're covered in blood." He presses his lips against my ear, his beer-tinged breath nearly making me puke. "Into kinky shit are you? This will be fun."

He kicks my legs apart. Pushing his arm across my upper back, his body weight holds me firm as he fumbles to get out his cock.

Now.

I push back against the wall and turn. Cock in his hand, he looks stunned that I'm free. But instead of attacking I lean back against the wall.

He shrugs and comes toward me cock first.

Grabbing his head, I position his neck and bite.

He shouts, but my venom quickly subdues him and he slumps forward over me.

Adjusting his body so the wall shares some of his weight, I lean against the bricks and concentrate on draining his blood.

Even tainted with alcohol and what tastes like a diet of fried food and microwaved garbage, his blood is delicious. If not delicious, then nourishing, life giving and exactly what I need.

As I gulp down the warm elixir, I feel my strength returning full force. How have I survived so many months without feeding straight from the vein? How have I grown used to the pale substitutes I was offered?

Heat and power flow through me, waking every cell and making me feel alive, as alive as I've felt since I was human. The rate of flow from his vein slows, but I continue to gulp.

My belly's full, but I want more.

If he's going to live, I have to stop—now. But does this rapist deserve to live?

I release my fangs to breathe and give myself a moment to decide. I lick rivulets of blood off my mouth and chin, making sure I don't waste even the smallest drop.

Even with him half-unconscious and near death, the man's breath makes me gag, its pungent odor overpowering the garbage smells that the rain released from the alley's pavement.

I want to kill him. I want to drain this creep of every last corpuscle in his body, but killing humans is wrong and completely taboo in the vampire world. I might not have learned much from other vampires, but I have learned that.

The few vampires who kill their victims are the ones who draw attention to our kind, the ones who make humans hate us, make our mere existence illegal.

Reluctantly, I lick the puncture wounds on his neck to seal them. When the asshole comes to, he'll have no memory of me, no idea why he's lying in an alley with his dick out.

Because no way am I putting that back.

Hidden behind his slumped body, I rest for a few moments, letting the man's blood nourish me. Even after taking so much, I could feed again, but I no longer *need* to. What I need is to find a safe, dark place to wait out the inevitable daylight.

The scumbag flies away from me, landing with a smash against a nearby dumpster.

Startled, I launch myself at whoever or whatever pulled the man off me.

"Don't be afraid," a deep male voice says as I collide with an impossibly large and hard body. "You're safe now. You're going to be okay."

Pinned by steel-band-like arms, I'm about to plunge my fangs into another neck—or chest, since I can't reach his neck—when I come to my senses and relax in the man's hold.

This man "rescued" me with no idea I didn't need the service.

My Good Samaritan strokes the back of my head as he holds my naked body against his massive one. "You're bleeding," he says with alarm.

"It's not my blood." I hope he won't ask for more explanation. "Let me down. Please?"

He sets me onto my feet and backs away quickly, facing down the alley instead of toward my naked body. "You need me to call an ambulance? The cops?"

"No." I grab the damp trench, put it on and wrap it tightly around me. "No cops. Please?"

He nods, his gaze still scanning the alley, staying off me. He's the tallest man I've ever seen, at least seven feet if I had to guess, and the massive expanse of his back and chest doesn't seem real. He's way bigger than even Pike.

His body shifts and the movement confirms that the

massive mounds under his T-shirt, wet from the rain, are pure muscle. No wonder he was able to toss my nearly empty meal container aside with such ease.

I find what's left of the coat's belt and tie together the pieces my would-be rapist cut with his knife.

"Thanks," I say. "I'm okay now. And dressed."

"You sure you're okay?" He slowly turns toward me, and light from above finds his features.

I gasp. It's probably the effects of the fresh blood in my system, but this man is the most attractive human being I've ever seen. In fact, he's the only human man I've ever found truly attractive. This man is handsome without a hint of pretty, and there's something rugged and unbelievably masculine about his looks. Like a model combined with a Viking.

His rain-soaked shirt clings to a well-sculpted body, and even damp from the rain, his wavy, thick hair, short on the sides and longer on top, is as blond as mine was before I dyed it—nearly white. His strong jawline sports sexy stubble. But the best part is, in spite of the man's rugged appearance, his light eyes—the color of a glacier-sourced lake—are filled with more genuine compassion and concern than I've had directed my way—ever.

He extends his arm toward me and the forearm hairs reflect the light like strands of gold, even without taking the rain droplets into account. If I hadn't just fed, I'd never be able to keep my fangs out of this man's neck, and I watch his vein pulse, almost as if his blood wants out, as if his blood *wants* me to feed.

He takes a step toward me, but stops an arm's length away.

His arm's length, which is much farther than I want him to be at this moment, or maybe ever again.

I know the danger. I know I can't let this human man discover who I am, *what* I am, or what really happened in this alley before he arrived, but after months of captivity, combined with the stress of escaping and the relief of feeding, all I can think about is seeking comfort in his arms.

"I'm a little shaken." I step toward him and he sucks in a sharp breath.

Stretching my arms around his body I lean against him. My hands don't come close to meeting behind his back, barely even reach past his sides, but he feels so strong and warm against me.

"Can you just hold me a minute?"

He exhales as his arms wrap gently around my body. Not in my entire life have I felt so safe, even though I'm anything but.

Under my ear, his heart rate increases, thumping through his chest. The sound is like a lullaby, rocking me, easing my tension and pain. I detect something unusual about it—almost like extra beats—and with each forceful push from his heart, the rush of blood in his veins sounds as powerful as a waterfall.

Intoxicated, I'm starving again, even though I just fed.

Have I forgotten what a human's heart and blood sound like? How it feels to be held? Have I ever really known the latter? After escaping my stepfather, I avoided men and the only person I ever let hug me was my friend Lark. My heart squeezes. I haven't let myself think of her in months.

"Let's go inside." His deep voice reverberates through my body.

I lift my head and turn toward the scumbag lying next to the dumpster. "Is he dead?"

My Good Samaritan leaves my side for a moment to

check the man's pulse. "He's alive. But if you want, I can make sure he never does this again."

Has he just offered to kill for me? "Just leave him," I say.

"He should be in jail..." His voice trails off, making me think he doesn't want to involve the cops any more than I do, and I suppose he doesn't want to get involved as a witness. Or is he worried he'll get arrested for assault? A man his size must worry about that kind of thing all the time.

I shake my head. "I just want to forget about him."

The big man turns toward me with a half grin, his eyes dancing with humor. "I suppose waking up with his ass in a puddle and his dick hanging out might teach him a lesson."

"He doesn't seem like the good-student type."

The man chuckles as he gestures with his head toward a door in the alley. "Come." He reaches back toward me. "Let's get you dried off and warm."

I follow, regretting that he drops his offered hand when I get close enough to take it.

"What's inside?" I ask, suddenly wary as he opens the heavy metal door.

"A bar. My bar." He shakes his head. "That asshole who attacked you was inside earlier. I kicked him out for saying something rude to my waitress. Tonight's the last time he gets a drink in this neighborhood." He holds open the door, and I step into a dimly lit hallway, painted black.

My night vision restored, I spot a door to my right, slightly ajar, with a staircase leading down. Ahead, a wood planked floor stretches along a hallway that's well worn but clean, considering it leads to the back door of a bar. The walls are freshly washed. I smell the lemon from the cleaning fluid and sense the residual dampness from when they were cleaned this morning.

Multiple voices and the thump of music waft down the hall. The sharp tang of ammonia mixed with urine hits my senses as I pass the men's room; the same comes from the ladies', and then finally the scent of beer, peanuts and human blood takes over as I step into the main room of the bar.

The wood plank flooring continues into the main room, where my savior ushers me toward a booth. Before sitting, he gestures for a waitress. She appears instantly.

"Ask Kev to cover for me behind the bar?" he asks her.

"Sure, boss," the waitress answers. "Can I get you something?"

He leans one hand on the table and I can't help but notice his fingers—long and thick, and dusted with blond hair.

In spite of my recent abuse by fingers, I can't help but find his digits sexy. Why am I so attracted to this man? A human, no less. And why am I still hungry?

"What can I get you?" he asks me. "On the house."

I shake my head. "I'm not much of a drinker." I slide onto the bench facing the entrance to the bar. I'd prefer a position where I can see both of the exits. But since I lack eyes in the back of my head, watching the front will do.

"Coffee? Hot tea?" He's not going to take no for an answer.

"Whiskey," I respond. "Irish if you have it."

Smiling with surprise, he nods, then taps the table with those sex sticks he likely calls fingers. "Whiskey it is."

He turns to the waitress. "Two Jamesons. Black Barrel. Better make them both doubles." He slides into the booth, sitting opposite me.

The man looks even better in this light, and the soft

warm glow sparks off his strong features, making me think of honey. Honey I'd like to lick off.

"What's your name?" he asks.

"Selina."

"Rock." He nods.

"Like a stone?"

"Like Hudson."

"The river in New York?"

He grins. "Rock Hudson. Actor from the 1950s."

"Okay." That's kind of random. "Nice to meet you, Rock." Glad for an excuse to touch him, I extend my hand to shake his, and his much larger one engulfs mine gently as he smiles.

But he lets go too soon. My fingers graze his palm, delighting in the calluses and mounds of muscle he has even there. You'd think my sex drive would be in neutral, at least for a while, but being a vampire is strange and still new to me. From the moment I spotted this man, my libido's been in high gear, likely made worse by the feeding.

"I noticed you don't have a purse," he says. "Were you robbed?"

I shake my head.

"Can I call someone for you?"

"Call someone?"

"A friend? Boyfriend? Husband? Do you have your phone on you?"

"No, I..." I try to remember all the cover stories I used with humans before I was captured. Frankly, I avoided human conversations—too much risk they'd suspect me and call the police or stake me themselves. "If it's okay, I'll just rest here a bit, warm up?"

"Stay as long as you need," he says. "And if you change your mind and want to borrow my phone, let me know."

I nod. "I'm fine. Really." I pull my hand down to my lap to hide its trembling.

The only thing I need is sleep—somewhere hidden from the sun, and from the cops and Pike.

I should find somewhere soon, but it's tempting to stay in this bar and close to Rock for as long as I can.

The waitress sets down our drinks, and he smiles. "Thanks, Chelle."

"No sweat." She walks away, shooting a heated look over her shoulder.

Clearly I'm not the only female in the room who finds Rock attractive.

If she touches him I'll kill her. My murderous thought catches me off guard.

"What is it?" he asks.

I shake my head.

"You smiled just then. Kind of a *wicked* smile if you don't mind my saying. What were you thinking about?"

"Nothing." I wrap both hands around my glass like it's an anchor. "I'm just grateful you came along when you did."

"Me too." He nods. "So, Selina." The way he says my name is unbelievably sexy, lingering on the long E sound—Seleeena. "What's your story?"

"It's a long one," I say, then immediately regret that I may have made him more curious. Even if I wanted to share my story, I can't. It's a matter of survival.

He shifts his large body, his legs spreading wide under the table. It's the sexiest thing I've ever seen.

"I've got time." His deep voice resonates, filling my body, filling the room.

Time. I want to spend time with this man. A lot of time. If only I had it.

If only I could talk to him freely, without him discovering I'm a vampire.

CHAPTER FIVE

Rock

The cute, purple-haired vampire takes a sip of her whiskey and then scans the room, clearly looking for danger. Her slight body is tense, ready to attack—or run—on a second's notice, and I don't want to do anything to trigger either reaction.

When I tossed that creep off her in the alley, I didn't expect to discover that *she* was the attacker, not him. Even if his intent was rape, she had the upper hand way before I arrived on the scene.

It's impossible to know who attacked first, but it certainly wasn't your typical vamp-feeds-off-a-drunk-in-an-alley situation. Not by a long shot. The guy's dick was out, and Selina was naked, blood trailing down her back and legs. She was clearly shaken. Terrified. There's more to Selina's story, and I have to know it.

Not in a hundred years have I wanted to know someone so badly. Even though we just met, part of me never wants to let her out of my sight. But I need to tread carefully, let her know that she's safe.

I've never met a vampire who seems so vulnerable, so innocent, and I want beyond words to protect her. She looks young—barely out of her teens—but with vamps, appearances are always misleading.

Her hair, though... It's the same color as the lilacs that grew outside the cave in Ireland where I spent a cold winter over eighty years ago. Such hair colors have only been common in the past decade or so, so her transition must be fairly recent.

"When you're ready to tell me what happened," I say softly. "You can trust me. I would never call the cops."

Her head lifts, like she might open up, and she smiles.

Both of my hearts skip a beat.

"There's not much to tell," she says in a way that proves the truth is the opposite.

Selina's skin is delicate, pale perfection, and her eyes, large in her tiny face, are the lightest blue, nearly silver, surrounded by the remnants of dark makeup that's staining her eye sockets and trailing down her cheeks.

My thumb twitches with the desire to reach across the table and wipe away the eye shadow remnants, to feel her skin that's undoubtedly soft.

She takes a long sip of her drink, closing her eyes in obvious enjoyment, and something stirs deep inside me. Not only is she beautiful, I really appreciate a woman who appreciates whiskey.

"How'd you end up in my alley?" I ask her gently.

She licks her upper lip, and I'm instantly hard at the sight of that tiny pink tongue.

Filling with shame, I shift on the bench. It's been

decades, many decades, since a woman's had that effect on me. Not since... I shake my head to banish the thought.

She glances up to the side. "I got locked out of my apartment."

I love that she can't keep eye contact while she's so obviously lying. I try to think of questions she might be able to answer truthfully. "Do you live nearby?"

"Not far." Her eyes dart around the room. "My roommate's probably home by now. She can let me in." She looks down at the table as one of her slender fingers traces the wood grain. "As soon as I feel a bit stronger, I'll get out of your hair."

"But look." I rake my fingers over my scalp. "You're not in my hair. See?"

She laughs softly at my corny joke, but as her smile fades her expression turns sad, making me want to leap over the table and take her into my arms.

I've never seen a vampire—a natural predator—so vulnerable, so guarded. Her eyes dart around the room once again. Someone or something has terrified this woman, and I'll bet it wasn't that asshole in the alley. Not *just* him.

My instinct to protect Selina overwhelms me, even though I know she must be strong enough to take care of herself.

Questions tingle on my tongue. I want to know everything about her, but she'll bolt if she suspects that I already know her most carefully guarded secret.

"You should call your roommate." I pull out my phone and offer it again.

She shakes her head. A lock of wet purple hair lands curled around her cheekbone and she pulls it off. "There's no point. She never picks up numbers she doesn't recognize."

Her lies are getting better, offered with more confidence.

"Any chance your roommate won't come home *at all* tonight?" I want her to stay here where she'll be safe.

Her lips twitch, but she shakes her head, then tucks damp waves behind a tiny ear. "She'll be home."

"You don't look very sure." I lean onto the table, wanting to get closer but not wanting to crowd her. I know how intimidating I am.

"Listen...I know you don't know me from Adam, but if you need a place to stay tonight, I've got a room downstairs. Nothing fancy. No window or anything, but it's comfortable and safe. Very quiet. No one will bother you. You could even stay all day tomorrow if you need the sleep. The bar will be closed."

I just described a vamp's dream room, hoping she'll bite—no pun intended. But I also described a serial killer's lair... Which way will she hear it?

Hope invades her eyes as she studies me, clearly trying to size me up. "Your offer is tempting."

My heart swells.

"I mean, what girl could turn down an offer like that? A man's dark, isolated basement, under a deserted bar? Doesn't sound dangerous at all."

Shaking my head, I lean back. "Look. You've got me all wrong. I would never—"

She grins. "I'm kidding." Her head tips to the side and the light strokes her cheekbone. It's like porcelain, marred only by streaks of eye makeup. "You don't seem like the serial killer type. You saved me in the alley, after all."

"You can trust me. Scout's honor." I hold up three fingers.

She draws in a quick breath and her pupils dilate. Is it

possible this gorgeous vamp is attracted to me? More likely I look like an attractive dinner. A massive feast.

Both thoughts stir the already hardening rod between my legs.

What the feck is wrong with me?

I would never lay a lustful finger on this woman, although my pecker *clearly* has a different opinion on that topic.

I draw a long breath, trying to ignore my desire.

Best I can do is show her that I mean her no harm. I'll behave as unthreatening as possible for a man of my size. After all these years, if there's one thing I've mastered, it's how to play the gentle giant.

CHAPTER SIX

Selina

The Irish whiskey softens the edge of the fresh human blood in my system, which already contained its fair share of booze. As far as I can tell, vampires don't get drunk, at least I don't, even after consuming about six times what would've made me pass out as a human.

Rock just offered me exactly what I need, a perfect solution to keep me out of sunlight until tomorrow night. But even though my gut says to trust him, everything about this guy seems way too good to be true.

I want to trust Rock. I want to trust him more than I've wanted to trust anyone in my entire life, but the last person I trusted was Santos and that mistake landed me in Xavier's brutal grasp.

But Santos was a vampire... I can defend myself against a human. If I had to guess, the big, blond man across the table outweighs me by a factor of three, but while he's got the size advantage, I've got the species advantage. Not that

I've ever tried to fend off or feed from anyone close to his size.

"So it's settled?" He leans back in the booth, his body making the wood creak as his face slides out of full light. Even partially shadowed, the huge man doesn't frighten me, although logic says he should.

I drain the rest of my whiskey. "Let's say I'm thinking about it."

"Sounds like progress to me." He nods toward the waitress.

"Why do you want to help me?" I ask, but I know the answer. He wants to help for the same reason any male has ever wanted to do anything for me—because he wants to fuck me.

"I don't know." He rubs his chin. "Typically when I rescue someone in the alley I just toss her out on the street. I'm kind of an asshole like that."

"I can't figure you out." I slide my hand across the wooden table. "But there's one thing I *am* sure of—you're not an asshole."

"Thanks." He tips his head to the side. "I think."

The waitress drops two more glasses of whiskey on the table and removes our empties.

"Thank you," I say and she nods, stone-faced. I'm not in the market for a female friend, but it's clear I haven't found a prospect.

"You coming back behind the bar?" she asks Rock.

"Kev too busy?" he asks.

"No." She shifts her weight onto one hip, jutting it out to the side and widening the gap between her T-shirt and her jeans' waistband. "It's just—"

"Let me know if it gets too busy, okay?" He smiles

broadly at her, and I swear I see her nipples harden under her gray tank top, like her body's reacting to his gaze.

"Sure, boss." She leaves and her butt sways in a way that must be intentionally provocative.

But it's more than a little satisfying to realize I'm the only witness to Chelle's performance from our table. Out of my peripheral vision I see that Rock's eyes are fully focused on me.

"Have you always lived in the city?" he asks.

I shake my head. "How about you?" Better to get him talking about himself. Men like that.

"No, me neither."

"Where are you from?" I tip my glass toward him. "You have a bit of an accent."

His eyebrows raise just enough to let me know my question pushed some kind of button. "I don't have an accent."

"Okay... So, if not Toronto, where are you from?" His accent definitely carries a hint of something—at least sometimes—but I can't tell what.

"Nowhere in particular," he says. "How about you?"

Seems like I'm not the only one evading questions. "I grew up in a small town. So small you haven't heard of it."

"Try me," he says. "I've been a lot of places."

"Like where?"

Chuckling, he shakes his head. "Before landing here, I traveled all over."

"Wanderlust?"

He shrugs. "I guess so." But his body language and expression tell me there's more to the traveling. Way more.

"Army brat?"

"Excuse me?" He leans back, hands on the table.

"You've never heard the expression?"

He shakes his head.

"It's what you call kids of military parents who dragged them all over the planet."

"That's not me." He casts his eyes down. "I don't even remember my parents."

"Oh, I'm sorry." Instinctively, I reach across the table and place my hand over his.

Staring at my fingers, he draws a long breath, then his hand flips to take mine.

And when I say *take*, I mean TAKE. His huge hand consumes mine, and warmth radiates from the point of contact to spread everywhere else in my body. The connection's beyond electric, like our conjoined hands contain a beating heart all their own, pumping desire through both of our bodies.

Our gazes meet, and I suck in a sharp breath.

Suddenly, the air in the bar is thicker, hotter, and the distance between us is charged. I've never felt so tempted—tempted to take him up on his offered room, tempted to share all of me: my secrets, my fears, my body, myself.

I've felt plenty of lust since becoming a vampire, most of it unwanted, but this is different—scary and comforting all at once. I want to set up house *inside* this man, to be part of him and make him part of me. For the first time, it's more than just arousal. But I feel that, too. I genuinely want to make love with this human. If only I could take the risk.

My heart gallops like it hasn't since before I transitioned, and the music playing in the bar dissipates, replaced by the sound of my breathing, of Rock's breathing, not to mention the rush of his blood gushing like a mountain stream in the springtime, one I want to drink from, bathe in, drown in.

I pull my hand out of his.

He gasps. "You okay?"

Cheeks heating, I nod. "Sure. But I really have to go. What time is it? My roommate's going to be worried."

Sadness fills his eyes, but he nods. He slides out of the booth and stands, his huge height taking me again by surprise. "I'll walk you home."

I shake my head. "That's okay. I'll be fine." I slide out of the booth and check that my coat's still securely wrapped around me.

"You can't leave like that."

"Like what?"

"Wearing nothing under your coat." His cheeks flush. "Let me get you something to wear. Wait here. Please."

He said *please* like his life depended on finding me clothes, on my accepting his help. How can I say no? Gripping the edge of the table to support me, I nod.

He heads down the hall toward the back door, and I perch on the edge of the bench, facing out from the booth, watching for danger as I drain the final ounce of my second whiskey, loving how the alcohol tickles my tongue and rushes into my bloodstream even before I swallow.

Since I became a vampire, it seems like anything that touches my tongue, or anywhere on my skin, absorbs into my bloodstream instantly, like I can feel the osmosis happening as everything I taste or touch becomes part of me. But not everything, now that I think about it. This only happens with things my body wants, that it craves. And my body clearly craves Rock.

He returns, holding a small bundle of clothes, including a pair of running shoes. I glance at my feet, filthy from the rainy streets. I barely realized I was wandering the city barefoot.

"Here." He passes me the bundle. "Everything's going to

be too big, but at least it'll keep you covered. It was the best I could do from the lost and found."

"Thanks."

I feel his gaze on my back as I walk to the ladies room, then I set the clothes on the counter and glance into the mirror. That was one of the first vampire "facts" I quickly learned was a myth: I have no problem seeing my reflection —although I do have a problem with what I see now.

All the diamond clips are gone from my hair and it's dried into matted knots. And the makeup that Jordina applied twelve—fourteen—hours ago? It's a mess.

The bathroom soap, strongly scented with fake lavender and real chemicals, is little help with the black and blue glitter mess on my skin, but I remove as much makeup as I can, and then take off the coat. My body's smeared with dirt and Pike's blood.

I look like I've been through a battle, and I suppose I have.

I splash lukewarm water on my face, then use paper towels to wipe off the worst of the grime, and my body starts to relax for the first time in—in almost forever.

I'm far from safe—I still need to find a place to sleep and I'm being hunted by a sadistic vampire—but I'm no longer a prisoner at Xavier's court, no longer being held in a dungeon where I'm tortured nightly. The dangers of surviving the upcoming day in this city seem minor by comparison.

The T-shirt Rock gave me is about four sizes too big, but it's clean and soft and has what I assume is the name of his bar on the front: O'Malley's.

Is that his last name? Is he Irish? Was that the hint of the accent I heard?

The sweat pants are less clean, less soft, and must have

come out of the lost and found like he said, but I manage to secure the drawstring waist tightly enough that they'll stay up. The runners are also too big but they'll work—at least until I get out of the bar.

My feet are fine bare, my skin much stronger than it was when I was human. It would take something very sharp to cut my skin, and even then I'd quickly heal, but I get that it looks strange to be running around the city barefoot.

The trench coat is filthy and stinks of the alley, but it might prove useful, so I slip it back on over the borrowed clothes and then thread my fingers through my hair, tidying it as best as I can without a brush.

Rock's right outside the restroom, his size filling the hall.

My heart skips and my belly flutters. What the hell is wrong with me? I just met this man.

"Everything fit okay?" he asks.

"Tailor made." I tug at the extra fabric at my hips.

The right side of his mouth quirks up, then he gestures for me to go ahead of him back into the bar.

"What's this song?" I ask, loving the slow rhythm, the strong horn section and the silky, deep quality of the singer's voice.

"It's vintage Al Green," Rock answers.

"Who?"

"Soul singer from the 1970s."

"Oh. Cool."

"'Let's Stay Together.'" He smiles.

I stop short and my belly swirls, my skin heats. I shake my head. "I told you. I have to go home."

"No. Um." He rakes his fingers through his blond waves. "That's the name of the song. It's a classic."

"Oh." I laugh. "Cool song. I like it."

"Me, too." He smiles and we look into each other's eyes.

Time stops as the music combines with the clinking and crashing sounds of the bartender cleaning up behind the bar. For the moment, there's nothing in the universe except Rock and the promise of safety I see in his eyes. For the moment, I believe I belong here, belong with Rock, that I've finally found a place in the world where I belong.

I turn away, unable to bear the hope.

Rock follows me to the door, and as soon as I get outside, I turn toward him. "I'm good from here. Thanks for all your help."

"Selina." His fingers brush the fabric of my coat sleeve, and the light contact sends waves of electricity coursing through me. "Please," he says, low and deep, "let me make sure you get home safely."

I shake my head.

"Then promise you'll come back. Promise that I'll see you again." He swallows hard, like his mouth and throat are dry. "I can't explain it," he says, "but I need—I need to see you again."

I need to see him again, too, even though I know it's risky.

Sooner or later he'll figure out what I am, and when he does, he'll either stake me himself or make sure the cops do. And even if Rock doesn't turn me in, someone else at his bar will. Probably the waitress.

It's beyond risky for me to see Rock again.

"Okay," I say softly. "I'll come back tomorrow night. I promise." And part of me actually means it.

~

Selina

WALKING AWAY FROM ROCK, I resist the urge to look back. When I left, the clock behind his bar read ten after two, but it's late spring so the sun will rise in about three hours. That doesn't give me a ton of time.

I can barely imagine how easy it must have been for vampires back when most humans thought our existence was a myth. How amazing it must have been to move freely through the night, taking just enough blood to survive without leaving any trace—no wounds or memories—before retiring to safe houses to shelter from the sun.

Even without a Maker to guide me, I've figured out a lot about how this whole vampire thing works, but I don't know the history. Still, it seems like humans and vampires once had—or must have had—a symbiotic relationship.

If it weren't for the rare vamps who drain their victims, like the one who bit me, humans and vampires might have continued in harmony forever, even after humans had proof we existed.

A shiver traces through me along with the sense that I'm being followed.

Is it Pike?

It can't be. If it were him, I'd already be dead, or more likely wishing I was.

Dodging the glow of a streetlight, I stop and press myself against the brick wall of an old warehouse that's been converted into condos. I scan the area. The brief hint of a shadow moves a block and a half behind me, but as I wait, trying to control my heart rate, there's no further movement. It could have been my imagination. Or a rat.

Earlier, while looking for my meal, I ruled out most of my old hiding spots. It's time to get creative.

I head toward some buildings on Sterling that used to be empty, but they're not empty anymore. In fact, one of them is an art gallery. The next building looks more promising.

I easily scale the fence at the back. Jumping over the barbs at its top, I land in a parking lot. Two rusted-out cube vans loiter in the corners.

Approaching the building, I peer through the iron bars of a basement window.

A pale face appears.

I jump back. Someone grabs me from behind, trapping my arms at my sides, tightening theirs around me like a boa constrictor. I twist, expecting to easily free myself from what I assume is a human, but I can't. My captor is definitely not human.

A male vampire steps into view, and he leans on a slim black cane with an ornate brass handle. He's wearing a huge curly brown wig and is dressed like he thinks we live in another century. He sports a lace scarf at his throat, an ornately trimmed velvet jacket, and pants that are tight over his calves, above high-heeled shoes tied with ribbons.

"Which syndicate, darling?" His teeth flash white in the moonlight.

"I don't have a syndicate."

He raises his cane and removes the rubber tip to reveal a sharp point. A sharp wooden point. After making sure that I see his stake, he slowly drags the point up from low on my belly, to stop just over my heart. "Pretty little thing like you? With no protection?" He shakes his head.

I raise my chin. "I can take care of myself."

"Doesn't look like that to me."

The vampire holding me from behind laughs in my ear. "I know how to take care of her." He dry humps my butt.

I'm desperate to get my body away from him, but don't dare move much, given the spike at my heart.

I fight to slow my heart rate, hoping to hide my fear. But if I let myself take too deep a breath, the spike might pierce my skin. It's already poked a hole in the T-shirt.

"Look," I say. "I don't want any trouble. I'm just looking for somewhere safe to spend the day. Cops were parked outside my usual place."

"Poor baby." The vampire exaggerates a pout. "Please. Let me be of service." He lowers his stake, steps forward and traces the back of his hand along the side of my face. "I don't ask much of my members, and my syndicate will protect you."

"Thanks, but I'm good." Except for the fact that the thug behind me is still holding me captive.

"*Are* you good?" he asks with lust in his voice. "I think I'll be the judge of that." Eying my neck, he reveals his fangs.

But instead of biting me, he steps back quickly, glancing around and sniffing the air. "Are you alone?"

I nod.

"Being followed?"

"No." My heart rate triples.

"She's bait. It's a trap!" The elegant vampire gestures with his cane.

I'm released, and the two vamps disappear into thin air. Even with my vampiric sight and reflexes, I barely saw them race away.

I scan the area for whatever or whomever they saw. Close to the next building, a shadow moves on the other side of the fence, but even my night vision can't detect what made that shadow, and I'm no longer sure I saw anything.

My tired, paranoid mind is playing tricks, and based on the way those vamps scattered, I'm not the only one feeling paranoid.

The lot has rundown, warehouse-style buildings on all sides, and I scan every inch of my surroundings, trying to sense danger and select another basement window to test. I need to find a place to sleep fast.

My nose lifts to sniff. I'm *not* alone. Humans. Somewhere within a few hundred yards.

I wait, watching, listening, but can't pinpoint where they are. Probably a group of homeless people or drug addicts have laid claim to one of these empty buildings.

When I was a teen, living on the streets, I often sought shelter in buildings like this for the night. That experience helped me survive after I turned, even though the time of day I needed shelter had been swapped.

The face of the vampire who drained me flashes in my memory and I shiver. Well-dressed in a tailored linen outfit with asymmetric lines, the female vamp tricked me into thinking she was an art gallery director—a human one. When she offered to give me career advice, I didn't hesitate to follow her for an instant.

Big mistake. Huge.

I hope I didn't make another tonight, by refusing to go with those vamps. Or running when they scattered.

Maybe life in a syndicate wouldn't be so bad. Most of the stories I know about syndicates came from humans, not vampires, and could be rife with bias. On the other hand Xavier's court was *worse* than I could have imagined.

I'm better off on my own. Always have been. Always will be. I can take care of myself.

With a loud bang, a million spotlights turn on me at once, and I hear and feel the rush of a dozen humans closing in from all sides. How did they sneak up on me so quickly?

Blinded by the sudden lights, as bright as the sun, I

jump and lunge, flailing around and hoping to strike some of the humans, or at least make my heart a more difficult target for their stakes.

Through squinting eyes, I spot a policeman in full riot gear, his spike aimed and ready and pointed toward me.

I leap, landing in a low crouch, then kick upward to knock the stake out of his hand. Spinning, I slam my fists into his chest.

He falls on his ass but looks unharmed, and my hands tingle from striking what felt like titanium on his chest.

Sensing another human behind me, I jump up and over her, just as she lunges. Her stake strikes the gravel. She tries to turn, but I kick her down, then toss her body across the parking lot.

I can defend myself from three or four wooden-stake-wielding humans at a time, but there are at least ten more alongside the two I've already tackled. I'm badly outnumbered.

If those vamps return, I'll gladly join their syndicate.

Two cops lunge at me at once. I leap about four feet into the air and kick each in the chest. They land on their asses, then roll across the gravel like bowling balls.

Another cop attacks from my right, wielding what looks and smells like a silver lasso. I spring out of his lasso's way, then dive for the man's legs, throwing his body high and off to the side.

Someone else comes from the front, catching me off guard, and I grab his stake mere inches from my chest. Using my other hand, I slam up and break the weapon in two, but he pulls another from his belt.

Is this it? Did I survive fourteen months in Xavier's dungeons only to die hours after my escape?

The gravel shakes underfoot and a huge roar fills the parking lot.

The cops turn toward the noise, giving me the opportunity to slam two of their heads together, knocking both of them out, even with their helmets.

Riot-gear-clad bodies fly through the air, some smashing into the walls of warehouses, and I turn in the direction the bodies are coming from.

Rock.

He seems even bigger and taller now than he did back at the bar, and he tosses police officers aside like toys, thundering in a rage-filled scream. As he runs toward me, each footfall shakes the earth so hard it must register on the Richter scale.

"Rock!" I barely get his name out of my throat before one of his huge arms scoops me off my feet and tosses me over his shoulder in a fireman's hold.

His long strides cover what seems like twenty feet at a time. Then we're in the air, wind rushing in my ears.

After clearing the fence, we land, and his body absorbs the impact so well I barely feel it. Lifting my head from his back, I spot the police readying their non-vampire weapons.

"Run!" I yell. "They've got guns!"

Shots reverberate, but Rock and I are already a block away, and then another, and I can only imagine that from the humans' perspectives we disappeared in a flash.

From the humans' perspectives.

I repeat the thought in my mind while I hold onto Rock's body, trying to keep the bouncing to a minimum as he runs. His back's so broad I have to grab on to what I can only assume are ridges of muscle at his sides.

No way is Rock human, and I remember how strange his heartbeat sounded.

He slows, and I loosen my death grip on his body.

"Hey," I say. "You can let me down. We lost them."

He slows to a normal pace, and then gently helps me down to the ground, keeping his hands securely on my waist when I land, like he fears I might bolt. He's not wrong to think that, but I'm too curious to leave.

We both pant, trying to catch our breaths as we stare into each other's eyes under the yellow-tinged light of a convenience store's neon sign.

"Did you follow me?" I ask.

"I'm sorry."

"Don't be sorry." Reaching up, I brush back a curly lock of blond hair from across his forehead. "You saved my life."

"If anything happened to you..." His voice trails off almost like he's choking back emotion.

Our eyes meet again and everything inside me lights on fire. Lights on fire with the desire to be in his arms for as long as he'll hold me, preferably forever.

In his eyes, I can view the ocean, behold the daytime sky that I now barely remember. In his eyes I can see the entire world. And it's a world I want to live in. A world where I might find peace and comfort and safety.

Rising up to my toes, I pull down on his head and press my mouth against his. I lick lightly, loving the lingering taste of whiskey and the salt of his sweat.

Our mouths press together, neither of us moving. And that's okay with me. I can stay like this forever. The sounds of the city have gone; there's only our trembling lips, our bodies' heat and our comingling breaths.

A moan rumbles up from deep inside Rock and it shakes his entire body. His lips vibrate as he exhales against mine, warming my face, my body, my soul. Lifting me into his arms, he captures my lips with unmitigated passion. One hand on my head, the other clasping my waist, he spins me around as he holds me tightly, and it feels as if our kiss has lifted us both off the ground, not just me.

The entire world disappears, evaporates in the heat generated by our hungry kiss, and I've never felt so alive, so present, yet in a dream at the same time. Every one of my vampiric senses is completely consumed by our kiss, by the taste of Rock, the smell of him, the feel of him hard against my body.

My life, my whole world is Rock now, and I won't survive if this kiss ever ends.

The spinning subsides and a brick wall presses into my back, his hand cushioning my head as he continues to kiss me.

Yes, I think. Yes. This is my life now. Kissing Rock. Forever. This is how I want to stay for the rest of my life.

He pulls abruptly away, his breathing heavy as he looks into my eyes with so much desire it multiplies my own.

"We need to stop," he says. "I can't..."

I fight to catch my breath, to find words, to let my heart rate come down, and most of all to kill my impulse to dig my fangs into his neck.

Within striking distance, Rock's blood courses through him with the power of Niagara Falls, and there's something else... Two heartbeats?

I exhale. Hard.

"What are you?"

CHAPTER SEVEN

Selina

Rock opens his mouth like he's going to answer my question, then his expression changes and he urgently glances around us.

"Someone's watching," he whispers. "Another vampire."

I gasp, hearing the words on his lips. *Another*?

He knows what I am.

Or is he referring to the two vampires I encountered earlier? Was Rock watching me then?

"Let's get out of here." He pulls me off the wall and starts to run with me in his arms.

"I can run fast too," I say as I cling to his side, my legs trying but failing to circle his ribs.

"I know," he says, but he doesn't set me down, and I don't complain.

The city blocks blur past as he carries me.

As fast as he is, at my top speed I'm much faster, but I love feeling his hard body against mine as he uses it like a powerful machine to transport us. Of course, if a vampire was watching us, he or she could overtake us easily. It can't have been Pike or I'd already be caught.

Unless... unless whoever was watching is afraid of Rock.

Should *I* be afraid of Rock?

I press my nose near his neck, inhaling his mysterious and intoxicating scent and fighting to keep my fangs in check. He smells different than any man I've encountered, more like the earth, the forest, the air. But it's not like I've deliberately smelled any men.

Before I turned, the only man who was ever this close to me was my stepfather, and with him I'd breathe through my mouth to minimize his stench. After my transition, I only had my face this close to my meal containers, and I'm not positive how non-drunk human men smell.

As he runs, my body undulates in anticipation, and I'm so hungry—hungry for him—that I'm about to burst.

I lick his neck.

"Not now, Acushla," he murmurs in my ear. "Everything in good time."

Acushla. I have no idea what that means, but love the sound of it. And even more I love the intimacy of his calling me by a special name. I close my eyes, letting myself drink in long slow breaths of Rock, letting that be enough. Enough for now.

He doesn't set me down when he stops at the back alley door to his bar, but removes the hand that's cupping the back of my head to dig into his jeans pocket for the keys. He quickly opens the door.

We step inside and he carries me down a flight of stairs and across what looks like a storeroom. He pushes aside a huge, fully loaded shelving unit to reveal another door, which he unlocks and then carries me down another long flight of stairs.

At the bottom, I slide down his body, my thigh bumping over a huge lump of muscle. When my feet touch the ground, I stay close, pressed up against him, not ready to break our connection. I don't want the connection to break, not ever.

As he switches on a light, our bodies shift against each other. He groans.

I gasp. The hardness I felt under my thigh is now pressed against my torso. It's unmistakable. As I lean against him, it pulses, sending shivers of excitement and fear coursing through me. Is that really his erection?

He pulls away and holds me at arm's distance.

I try to resist looking down, but my gaze dips quickly to confirm what I felt, and it's even more staggering than I imagined. An impossibly thick bulge curves to the left and down, straining against the denim. It's got to be at least three or four inches across and extends halfway down his thigh. It's so long and double the girth of any cock or dildo that's violated my body.

Lust and fear battle inside me. I need to make love with Rock more than I need air or blood, but he's so big.

"I'm sorry," he says.

I look up into his eyes and they're filled with more pain than I can imagine. And I'm very familiar with pain.

His constrained erection must be uncomfortable, and I tell myself to be brave. I reach toward his fly, but he catches my wrist.

Looking up into his eyes, I realize it's not just pain that I see, but shame. Shame that he's *aroused*?

"It's okay," I say quashing my fear. "I want to do this." And I want to believe my own words. I've never had consensual sex, and while I hoped that some day I'd have sex without pain, making love to Rock will be worth the inevitable discomfort.

I want, more than I need blood, to make Rock feel good, to see pleasure and desire take the place of the shame in his eyes.

Rock would never hurt me. Not like all those vampires who came before him.

I twist my arm in his grip until we're holding hands. Then I raise our clasped fingers to kiss his huge knuckles, one by one. Looking into his eyes, I circle his index finger knuckle with my tongue.

He sucks in a ragged breath. "No, Acushla. We can't."

"Acushla," I whisper. "What does that mean?"

He smiles softly, through his obvious discomfort—clearly fighting lust. "Acushla means...it means pulse of my heart."

"Oh!" My heart flutters. "How beautiful."

That's how he sees me? Even if it's just a generic term of endearment, like how some men call women *baby*, I love it. And the way he said it to me didn't sound generic.

"Forgive me." He steps back. "But I need a moment alone. Please."

I hold onto his hand until our arms are completely outstretched between us. Then our fingertips brush slowly as he peels his away. He crosses the room and disappears behind a door at the far end.

And what a room it is. Although we're two stories underground, the ceiling is at least ten feet high, and it's cozy down here, and somehow the air is fresh. The walls are painted in a golden-hue—like an egg yolk—that complements the mostly oak furnishings, some of which are clearly expensive antiques, as beautiful as the ones at the big museum on Bloor.

The faint sound of a shower comes softly from behind the closed door and I smile to myself. After all the exertion, he wants to clean up for me before sex.

I wouldn't mind a shower myself. Should I join him?

That seems too forward. He asked for a moment alone, and as attracted as I am, now that I've gone a few minutes without touching him, I realize I've been stupid to fully trust him. I don't even know who he is—or *what* he is for that matter.

And that thick bulge has left me both excited and frightened. Anticipation spreads through my body, then gathers back in a tight squeeze between my legs. My sex pulses as I wait for him, my wetness and expectation both building.

To distract myself, I run my hand over the top of a glass-front bookcase. It's got a simple design, but at the same time it's one of the most beautiful pieces of furniture I've ever seen. Dozens of books rest under the glass, tightly packed, some of them with what look like leather covers. I hope to get a chance to explore the reading tastes of this mysterious man, or whatever he is. But right now, it's not his books I most want to explore.

An oversized sofa, covered in well-worn leather, and a massive red leather armchair sit in the middle of the room, and I turn back to the staircase wondering how he got these huge pieces down here.

Several striking paintings hang from the walls, large canvases with abstracts painted in graphic colors. The images draw me forward, like they're inviting me into their world.

One that's painted in greens and purples and blues

immediately gives me an intense feeling of peace and safety, and I stare at it for a long time, letting the calmness tame my lingering fears.

The next painting, in slashes of reds, yellows, blacks and grays, instantly sends a chill to my bones. These aren't IKEA prints, they're originals, and I don't recognize any of the artists. None of the canvases are signed, but clearly Rock is an art collector. Real art. And he has a lot of original pieces and collectables for a man who seems relatively young—under thirty if I had to guess.

I count at least six side tables and chests, and atop or inside each are exotic objects, but the excess of knickknacks doesn't come off as clutter, it adds to the coziness.

I run my fingers over an old-timey circus tent, fabricated out of what seems to be painted tin. It looks very old, the paint worn in places, and when I touch the flag at the top I realize the entire tent spins.

"Do you like that?" Rock's voice rumbles from behind me, and I turn to find him dressed in a simple T-shirt and jeans that now lack the obvious bulge.

I can fix that.

"You have some beautiful things."

"Thanks." He comes up beside me, and I immediately feel warmer, not even realizing I was cold.

He twists the flagpole between his thumb and forefinger, and as the tent spins the sides rise to reveal an intricate scene with small tin figures, including a lion and his tamer, three clowns, a tightrope walker, plus a full audience.

"Wow. That's incredible. Where did you get it?"

He steps back and looks away. "Memento of a time I'd rather forget." His voice tightens.

"I'm sorry."

He shakes his head as he crosses the room, then he

gestures toward the sofa. "Sit. Please. Can I get you another whiskey?"

"Sure."

I curl into the sofa, legs tucked up underneath me as he pours our drinks and returns.

"Thanks." I take mine and pat the cushion beside me.

But instead of taking my hint, he moves over to the big chair and sits, filling it completely. "You okay?" he asks.

I nod, suddenly nervous. Am I foolish to trust him?

"Who are you running from?" he asks.

I lean back against the cushions. "Seems to me, I'm the one who needs answers. *What* are you?"

"You go first."

The sexy vibe in the room turns off like a switch as we eye each other with an entirely different kind of interest.

His huge hands slide along the arms of his chair and then grip the leather, his fingers digging in deeply before relaxing. "You have no reason to be frightened," he says. "I would never hurt you."

"How do I know that?" My voice doesn't come out as strong as I'd like. Suddenly I feel vulnerable, alone. And frightened. I hate that.

He runs his hand through his hair, still damp from the shower, then slowly shakes his head. "Best I can do is tell you the truth."

"And what truth is that?" I'm in his basement, lured down here by lust and a false sense of safety. For all I know he's about to kill me. Or worse. I am very familiar with worse.

"Let's start with this," he says softly. "How about I tell you what I know about you?"

I stiffen. "You don't know *anything* about me."

"I know that you're frightened. I know someone's chasing you. And I know *what* you are."

Fear grips me like a straight jacket formed from silver, and I press back into the corner of the sofa. "Are you working for him?"

"For whomever's chasing you?" His expression is horrified. "No. I don't even know who that is, except that it's a vampire. A powerful one, if I had to guess. More powerful than that dandy who confronted you earlier."

"Dandy?"

He shakes his head to dismiss my question. "How long have you been a vampire? Who turned you? Why aren't you still under the protection of your Maker? Or a syndicate?"

I suck in a sharp breath. I suspected that he'd figured out my secret, but to hear all of it confirmed so bluntly... Rock has all the power at this moment, and I hate that.

I straighten. "Your turn. You know what I am. What the hell are *you*, because you sure aren't human."

He draws a long breath, then leans forward in his chair, the leather and wood creaking under his weight. "You're right. I'm not human."

"Then what?"

"A giant." He looks down. "Or part giant, I think."

"You *think*?" I blink, waiting for him to say more. "A *giant*? Like Jack and the Beanstalk?" Sounds like bullshit.

"Giant is the only thing anyone's ever called me. I never met my people. I already told you I never knew my parents."

"You *never* knew them? Not *at all*?" I ran away from mine at an early age and with good reason, but I can't imagine how lonely it would feel to not even know who either of my parents were. At least I knew my mom.

He folds his arms, almost hugging himself. "My first

real memories are from when I worked in a circus. That was the only life I knew—for decades. I don't even have flashes from any life before that."

"Decades?" I was wrong. He's older than thirty.

"I was a main attraction in one of the biggest traveling freak shows to come out of Ireland."

"I *knew* you were Irish." I try to swallow a smug smile.

He shrugs. "Thing is, I don't think I *am* Irish. I looked about ten when I joined the circus—so the others told me—and when I joined them I didn't know a word of English—or Gaelic. My friends guessed I was from one of the Scandinavian countries but I didn't speak any of those languages either."

"You didn't speak at all?"

"Oh, I spoke. Just not in a language anyone else could understand."

"Wow." I relax and turn, absorbing this as I lean back against the sofa's arm and stretch one of my legs along its back. I take a small sip of whiskey.

"When was this?"

"Late eighteen hundreds."

I choke on my whiskey, narrowly avoiding a spit take. "What? You're, like, well over a hundred years old?"

One side of his mouth quirks up. "Yup. So you'd better learn to respect your elders, young lady." He wags his finger, then the moment of joking vanishes from his expression as he leans forward. "At least I assume I'm your elder. How long ago were you turned? How did it happen?"

"Less than two years ago and..." *And I have no idea how it happened. At least, not the transformation part.*

"So recent. You're so young..."

I frown. "I am not *that* young."

"In vampire terms you are." He closes his eyes for a

moment. "And I..." He drags a whistling breath through his lips.

"What?"

"Knowing your age, I'm even more glad that I..." His smile turns patronizing. "Wow."

"Glad of what?" I straighten my back, coming out of my sofa slump.

"I'm fecking glad I didn't let that kiss go any further."

My cheeks heat as anger and disappointment swirl inside me. Reducing what happened between us to the word *kiss* seems insulting. And I don't like him treating me like a child, his inferior.

"What makes you think I would have *let* it go any further? Maybe I was just luring you in so I could feed on you? Maybe I still plan to."

He raises his palms toward me in surrender, but he's still looking at me like I'm a child.

"I could do it, you know. I'm very strong."

"I have no doubt."

I stand, rising at a speed humans can't detect. Then I leap onto the ottoman near his feet. "You don't believe me."

He looks up at me, tipping his head to the side and exposing his vein. "Drink if you're going to."

His submission fuels my indignation. "I'm not hungry. Besides, giant blood smells rancid."

His head straightens quickly, and hurt flashes in his eyes.

"Thanks for the whiskey." I drop the empty glass and it smashes on the stone floor at the edge of the carpet. "I'm out of here."

"That was Waterford," he says as I cross the room.

"What?" I turn back.

"Waterford crystal. A long-ago discontinued pattern. Can't be replaced."

Twinges of guilt and embarrassment shoot through me. "So what? I'm a freaking vampire. I do what I want." I head for the stairs, but he beats me there, blocking my escape route with his bulk. How did he move so quickly?

"Let me go." Panic creeps into my bravado. Maybe his giant story wasn't total bull.

Maybe I am captive here. Maybe he plans to eat me after he punishes me with that monstrous cock.

"You can't leave," he says.

A far too familiar switch flips inside me. I leap forward, clawing at him, trying to get past him and up the stairs. "Let me go. Let me go. Please. I can't be a prisoner again. Let me go. Please."

"Selina." He holds me tightly, his arms like steel bands as he lets me rail against him, his hard body absorbing each blow. "It's dawn. You can't go outside."

I continue to fight, but the reality of his words sinks in. Even if he does plan to torture me, to rape me, to kill me, I'm stuck here. I can't leave. Not for the next fourteen hours or so, anyway. Spring at this latitude sucks for vampires.

As I relax in his arms, his hold turns gentler, and in spite of myself I start to sob. There are no tears, that's the one bodily fluid that disappeared after my transition, but every other part of my body lets loose, the stress and adrenaline that built up through my months of captivity, for years before that, all release at once.

Rock strokes my back, absorbing my pain. When I calm down, he carries me back to the sofa, setting me down in one corner and then claiming the other, keeping some distance between us.

He remains quiet, calm, letting me recover and not

pushing or coddling me in any way. Looking into his eyes is too intense, so instead I focus on the slow rise and fall of his massive chest, wondering where he gets clothes big enough to fit the wide expanse.

A giant. I've never heard of such a thing outside of fairy tales. If I feel alone, imagine how he feels if he's never known another one of his kind, if he's not even truly sure what he is.

I wipe under my eyes—an old human reflex. "When did you figure out that I was a vampire?"

His lips twitch. "The instant I pulled that rapist off you in the alley."

"Why didn't you say anything?"

"If I had, would you have let me help you?"

I shake my head.

He shrugs as if this is all the explanation required, and I suppose it is. I still don't feel as safe as I did earlier.

I know it would be smart to be cautious, but I wish I could get back to how I felt earlier. I wish I could kiss him, feel his arms around me, again. But you can't always get what you want. That's the one thing I know to be true.

What I felt earlier with Rock—the safety, the connection between us—it was too good to be true.

He's right that I can't leave while it's light, but sooner or later he'll go up to his bar. As soon as it's dark I'll make my escape.

CHAPTER
EIGHT

Rock

Fighting my body's urge to gather Selina into my arms, I press my back against the sofa, fearing I'll break the strong oak it's formed from.

Someone has hurt Selina, badly, and when I find him, I will crush him between my bare palms. I will grind his body into dust and sweep his remains into the sewer where it belongs.

"Who hurt you?" I ask softly. "Was it your Maker?"

She shakes her head.

I get another glass for her and pour us both more whiskey, leaving the bottle on the floor beside me.

"Sorry for breaking your glass," she says softly.

"Apology accepted."

"It was a childish reaction. I'm so embarrassed."

"No need."

She sips the whiskey, then runs her fingers through her tangled hair. "Is it okay if I take a shower?"

"Yes." I shake my head. "Sorry. Of course. I should have offered. I don't have any clothes that will fit you, but if you want something clean, help yourself to anything you can find. Bathroom's through there." I gesture toward my bedroom.

She smiles softly. "I figured that out."

Damned vampire hearing. Did she hear me in the shower? Hear the shameful thing I did there? But stroking myself to climax was the only way I could remove the danger of my desire. Desire like I haven't felt in nearly a hundred years.

I clear my throat. "There's a fresh towel on the shelf and soap in the shower—I don't have any fancy shampoo or anything."

"That's okay." She sets her glass on the floor and pads across the room, turning back at the bedroom door. "After I get cleaned up, I'll answer some of your questions. Okay?"

"Whenever you're ready."

She disappears into my bedroom and just the thought of her walking past my bed makes my pecker twitch and it threatens to stiffen again. Since I escaped the circus, the mere idea of my weaponized cock has been so revolting that every time I feel it tingle I've managed to stop it. Before tonight.

I haven't been stiff like that for decades—nothing beyond a hint of hardness I could calm with my mind as soon as it started—but tonight there was no other solution but hard strokes to remove my shame.

As soon as I laid palm to rod in the shower I came quickly and violently. Even after I tamed the monster, it's taken every ounce of concentration and control I possess to keep the damn thing from rearing its ugly head again—especially when I held her after her tantrum.

Selina is so frightened, and her attempt at bravery erupted as anger. I need to show her she can trust me. If she comes back from her shower to find my monster bulging against my jeans, it will not help set her at ease. I need to fight my brutish instincts and keep my cock tame. I thought the circus had cured my body of that affliction forever.

I shudder. I cannot, I *will not* let loose my sexual beast—never again—and especially not with Selina. Even if she has the ability to heal, unlike the other females I've ruined, I would tear her apart, and that would tear *me* apart.

I pace, trying to make a plan.

As I was trailing her through the streets tonight, I sensed another presence following her. But every time I tried to spot my fellow stalker, he vanished.

But I feel sure it was a vampire, and a male one, and it's clear that Selina needs help beyond what I'm qualified to provide. She doesn't even seem to fully understand what she is or all she can do.

Malcolm could help, but he can't travel in daylight and besides, I want her to trust me before introducing my powerful vampire friend. What if he wants another mate?

Rehearsing all the questions burning inside me and considering the least threatening way to ask them, I pace toward the stairs for what has to be the fortieth time since she left the room.

When I turn back around she's there, standing at the door to my bedroom, her lilac hair curling in damp tendrils over the shoulders of one of my T-shirts that hangs nearly to her shins. The sleeves are rolled up but the shoulder line rests close to her elbows.

As she passes by my art nouveau glass lamp, her face catches its light and her skin glows even more iridescent than the lamp's mother-of-pearl shade.

Selina is so beautiful. Objectively beautiful. And subjectively too. She's my absolute definition of beauty, especially now all the traces of makeup are gone.

And it's not just her beauty; she's beyond sexy, the most intoxicating combination of strength and fragility I've witnessed in my lifetime.

As she slowly advances, I run my hand over the stubble on my chin, watching her chest rise and fall with the force of her long slow breaths. Exhales I can imagine caressing my skin, my lips, my...

My lower body contracts as I expel a hard breath. Have I ever experienced desire so strong? This potent combination of sexual attraction and connection? This overwhelming desire to protect her, to possess her, to have her possess me?

I shake my head. I haven't felt desire like this since I was very young—if ever. I haven't allowed it.

For decades I convinced myself that I could shut down any hint of desire and hold my sex drive at bay, that I could intentionally shut down that part of me, but what I felt when I kissed her, what I'm feeling at this moment, exposes the notion of my self control as a fecking joke.

If we ever start kissing again... We cannot.

"I borrowed a shirt." She tugs down on the hem and the peaks of her breasts press against the fabric.

"I see that."

"Hope that's okay."

A smile grows from inside me. "It's perfect."

She lets the hem go, and all the air rushes out of my chest.

Strolling toward me, she scans everything she passes and drinks in my home in a way that fills me with pride, then she reclaims her spot in the corner of the sofa and picks up her discarded whiskey.

"Feel better?" I grab my glass and sit at the sofa's other end, turning slightly toward her.

Twisting to lean back and stretch her legs between us, she nods. "Much. Thank you. I couldn't wait to wash every trace of his..."

"Whose blood was it?" I ask after waiting a few moments for her to finish her sentence. I have so many questions that I have no idea where I should start.

Her eyes fill with fear and then hatred. But neither seems directed at me. She casts her gaze down.

"You can trust me, Selina. Let me help. Please. I can't explain it, but I want to help you more than I've ever wanted anything in my entire life." And I mean it. I want her to be safe and happy. "What happened to you?"

"It's a long story." Her face fills with pain.

I want to hold her, but it's too risky. Besides, I should give her space, let her come to me if she needs comfort as badly as I'm desperate to give it.

"Why don't we start with when you were turned," I say softly.

Drawing a long breath, she shrugs. "There's not much to tell about that."

I tip my head toward her, raising my eyebrows a little.

"I got attacked in an alley." She laughs sharply. "Just like tonight. You'd think I'd have learned to stay out of alleys by now, right?"

I raise my glass toward her, hoping she'll continue.

"It was the same day I dyed my hair purple." She twirls a lock of damp hair around her finger.

"That's why it stuck."

She leans forward over her perfect legs and rests her hands on her shins. “Is that why it stayed purple?” She shakes her head. “But I got my nails done that day, too, and the polish was gone in weeks.” She wiggles her tiny fingers.

“Nail polish doesn’t penetrate the cells. Hair dye does. But only if you dye it before you turn. If you dyed it now, it would only last a couple of days, at best.”

Her eyes narrow. “You know an awful lot about vampires.”

“And if I might say so, you *don’t.* Why didn’t your Maker teach you? Why aren’t you still under his protection?”

“Hers.”

My eyes widen with surprise. Beautiful young thing like Selina, I just assumed her Maker was male. But then again, sex isn’t usually the reason vampires make babies. They make them as allies, to gain power. But then why desert her?

Selina drains the rest of her whiskey. “You haven’t explained how you know so much about vampires.”

I lift the bottle to pour her more, but she holds her glass back. “There’s no point in trying to get me drunk, you know.”

I chuckle. “I know. But you seem to appreciate a good whiskey.”

“It’s delicious.” She licks the taste off her upper lip. “But that’s got to be pricey. I don’t want to waste it.”

“Lots more where this came from. I own a bar, remember?” I reach the bottle toward her and she lets me fill her glass before I top up my own.

“And don’t think you can distract me with this magical elixir.” She looks at me through the amber-liquid-filled crystal. “You still haven’t answered my question. Why do you know so much about vampires?”

"From a friend." I set the bottle on the carpet. "A vampire friend."

She sucks in a sharp breath and her entire body contracts in fear, her knees pull into her chest and her feet slide over the worn leather until she's almost in a ball. "Who do you work for? Which syndicate?"

I shake my head, looking directly into her very scared eyes and hoping mine will quell her fear. "It's not like that. My vampire friend, we met eighty, no, more like *ninety* years ago."

Her leg muscles relax a bit and she adjusts the T-shirt to hide the obvious fact she's not wearing panties.

My cock twitches in its confinement, refusing to stand down, and I hate myself for being aroused—especially now she's so vulnerable and frightened.

"My friend Malcolm is part of a syndicate here in the city," I continue. "More like a corporation than a syndicate, from what he's told me, but I've got nothing to do with them." Selina needs protection and Malcolm, or more likely his mate Astrid, can make sure she gets it. It's selfish of me to want to be the only protector she'll ever need.

And beyond the protection, Selina needs proper training, and while I can improve her fighting skills somewhat, there are things best learned from one of her own kind. Malcolm and Astrid can help Selina with that. If she'll let them. If she even lets me help.

Selina doesn't offer anything else, so I prod. "Your Maker. How soon after turning you was she killed?"

"Why do you think she was killed?" Her head tips to the side as if the thought had never occurred to her. "And she left *before* I turned. Bitch sucked me dry and left me for dead in the alley. I never saw her again."

I swirl the whiskey in my glass, giving her time to adjust this obvious lie.

When she doesn't, I lean forward. "That's not how it works, Selina. There's no way you could have turned without your Maker's help, especially if she nearly drained you."

She lifts her chin, slightly. "Well, that's what happened."

I frown, thinking it through. "And you were *human* when she drank from you."

She nods. "Very human. And happy." She glances down to her hands. "Truly happy for the first time ever. I was about to start a new job. And move into a new apartment with my friend... I had my whole life set and she ruined it."

"Your friend did?"

"No, my so-called Maker."

"None of this makes sense, Selina." I draw a long breath. If I accuse her of lying I might lose her trust again. "Okay. So, your Maker drained you and left you for dead. Given that, how can you even remember her? Her venom—"

"I know." She shrugs. "I don't get it, either. But I remember that night in vivid detail. I was chatting with a woman in a gallery, and I remember how sophisticated she was—or seemed—how generous and kind."

She frowns. "And I also remember how she pushed me against the wall the second we got into the alley. I can still feel the cold hard bricks against my back, and how the impact knocked the air out of my chest, how she grabbed my head and twisted my neck to the side." Her expression turns cold, angry.

"And I remember the searing pain when her fangs punctured my skin. And the intense pleasure that followed..." She shudders and her cheeks pink. "I remember how good it felt at first when she fed, how my entire body was bathed in pleasure, but then all of that changed."

She shakes her head. "I grew tired. So tired. And so desperate. I clawed and fought. Even as my mind grew foggy, I fought and fought. I tried to pull away from her fangs until the moment my pulse disappeared."

"Acushla..." My heart is breaking.

"I even remember how the ground felt when my shoulder struck it, then my head. I remember the smell of piss and oil in the alley, the light from a donut shop flashing in a puddle a few feet ahead of me as I watched her walk away, the red soles of her Louboutin stilettos reminding me of all the blood she'd drained from my body."

"You poor thing." The sound of Selina's voice, the look on her face... What she's describing isn't possible, but it's clear she believes that it's true.

"The transition itself was even worse," she continues. "So much worse. I..." She turns away. Her voice trails to nothing, and the pain on her face is more than I can bear.

"Listen." I stretch my hand across the back of the sofa toward her. "You don't need to tell me more. Not right now. Not if you don't want to. And my friend, Malcolm. He should hear this, hear you describe your transition. As a vampire, he might better understand how it happened."

Fatigue takes over her face, her body. It won't be long before she falls asleep and I mentally triage all the things I want to ask her before she does.

"Do you know who was stalking you tonight?"

"Besides you?" The side of her mouth quirks up.

I raise my glass toward her.

Her expression clouds, then she draws a breath so ragged it's like she's inhaling shards of glass. "His name is Pike. He's part of King Xavier's Guard."

"King Xavier?" I lean forward.

"So you don't know *everything* about vampires."

"Never said I did. Just that I'm friends with a few."

"King Xavier...he wanted me for a mate. But I couldn't." She shakes her head, determination rising on her face. "I *wouldn't* marry him. In revenge, he held me captive for fourteen months. And he raped me, tortured me, and then he let his Guard do it, too."

"Oh, my god." I reach forward to rest my hand on her shin.

To my utter relief and happiness, she doesn't recoil at my touch. On the contrary, she pushes onto her knees and falls into my arms. I cradle her against my chest as she curls her body into mine.

The strong connection I feel for Selina makes even more sense, now. I know what it's like to be captive, to be tortured and to torture others... Some instinct deep inside me must be drawn to her pain.

"I escaped his court," she says. "Just yesterday. But when I found a way out it was daylight, so I waited... I was so weak. I tried the door, five, maybe six times—burned by the sun each time. Then..."

She shakes her head against my chest and I bend down toward her, waiting for her to continue.

"You pretty much know the rest. It took hours for me to find someone to feed from. I was weak. I hadn't fed from the vein in almost a year."

Her breath warms my neck, her fangs within striking distance, and still I hold her. No chance would I *invite* her to feed from me, I know what that might lead to, but I won't stop her either. If she needs my blood to survive I will give her every last drop. With pleasure.

"And now..." Her voice fades. "Now, I'm just tired. So tired."

"Then sleep, Acushla. Just sleep."

Shifting, I turn to lift one leg onto the sofa and she adjusts as I slide it behind her.

I lean back and she falls asleep, her hair a lilac silk blanket draped over my chest.

CHAPTER NINE

Selina

I wake in the dark,pla but my night vision's fully working for the first time in a year, and I quickly recognize Rock's apartment, although my head's resting on a plush pillow instead of his hard chest.

As I sit, a thick warm blanket slides down my body to pool on the leather sofa beside me. I can't believe he got up without waking me. When did I last sleep so deeply? Have I ever? Even as a kid, I slept lightly, alert to the risk that my stepfather might come into my room.

Whether or not I should, I feel safe here. Safe with Rock.

"Hello?" I pad across the Persian rug. "Rock?" I reach his bedroom, and getting no response, I slowly open the door.

The bedroom's empty, his huge king neatly made, exactly how it was when I passed by it after my shower. Back in the main room I spot a huge plastic bag at the end of the sofa, half-hidden under the discarded blanket.

Curious, I check inside and discover it full of clothing, all in a size that makes it clear the clothes are meant for me.

I slip on a dress in soft gray jersey, which hangs loosely down to my knees. High necked and long sleeved, it's more on the Amish spectrum than my usual taste, but it's warm and comfortable and I like the idea that Rock bought it for me.

At the bottom of the bag are four identical pairs of sneakers in different sizes, five different styles of underwear and seven different bras. I giggle, imagining the giant man picking all of this out.

Since I already have the dress on, I decide to stay braless and slip on a bikini-style panty in a pale pink, then the size 7 1/2 black Keds. It's the second largest of the four size options he provided, and I sure hoped he kept the receipt for this stuff so he can return the wrong guesses.

Dressed, I head up the stairs. At the top, with my thumb ready to press down the old-fashioned tab of the door handle, I'm seized by a sudden panic. What if the door doesn't open?

Am I locked in here? Blocked in by that cabinet? Trapped, like back in the dungeon?

But the handle works, the door's not blocked and I step out into the storage area. Assuming this level is the same size and shape as those above and below, Rock sure must be storing a lot. Either that, or there's a hidden space on this level, too.

I discover a wall behind dozens of crates of alcohol and bar snacks, but no obvious door. I'm curious about the space behind the wall, but my desire to go upstairs and see Rock beats my curiosity, so I ascend the final stairs to the ground level and slowly ease open the door into the hallway that leads from the bar to the alley.

The only windows I spotted in the bar were painted over from the inside, but I was so tired last night, so rattled, that I'm not sure if I can fully trust my powers of observation.

Still, I can't detect any hint of sunlight coming from the bar, now. A scent—citrus combined with some kind of oily soap—fills my nostrils as I pad along the hallway and into the bar.

"Hey there, sleepyhead." Rock lifts his mop toward me. "You slept nearly thirteen hours."

"Guess I needed it. Thanks for letting me stay." The bar is empty except for us, and I was right about the painted-over windows. A tiny bit of sunlight permeates a small scratch on one window, next to the entrance, but other than that the light in the room is warm, fully artificial and safe. "Can I help you clean?"

"Nah." Rock grins and it makes the room feel even warmer. "I'm almost done."

"Thanks for the clothes." I half curtsey.

"Glad you found something there that works." He rinses the mop and leans the handle against the wall near the door. "Feeling better?"

I nod. "What time is it?"

"Six twenty. Staff will come in soon. We open at seven."

I did sleep a long time. Longer than I can ever remember. It was impossible to judge the passing of time in the dungeon, but I felt like I barely slept down there.

Leaving the pail and bucket near the door, Rock walks toward me and I fight the urge to dive into his arms. Now that he's near, his scent pushes aside the citrus cleaning supplies and makes me want to be surrounded by him. Consumed by him. To consume him, too.

"Listen." He rakes back his hair. "That vampire I told you about? Malcolm?"

Tensing, I nod.

"As soon as it's dark, he and his wife are coming by. Hope that's okay. I can call him to cancel."

Rock is less than two feet away from me now, and his scent, like the woods and the mountains, overtakes my thoughts so fully it's hard to even consider his question.

I close my eyes and inhale him, and as I drink in his scent, the rush of his blood fills my ears. Now that I'm rested and fed, my senses are back in full working order, and I can't believe I missed his double heartbeat at first.

It makes total sense that such a large body would need more than one engine to run it—or at least one huge and powerful one. And speaking of large organs, my eyes brush down over his body.

As if he knows where I'm looking and why, he shifts his hips and his hands cross over his body, hiding my opportunity to study his bulge.

His expression shows shame when I look up into his eyes.

"It's okay," I tell him. "I trust you." It feels good to say the words. It feels good to mean them, to be near him, and I wish I hadn't fallen asleep so quickly last night. A slight smile warms my lips and heats my body as I imagine what might have happened between us, what I hope will happen soon.

My strong vampiric libido is fully awake. I know I should feel an aversion to sex after so many months of torture, but my body no longer operates on human terms.

Even after I escaped my stepfather, the idea of sex remained repulsive. But since my transition my body's wanted sex—all the time—even though my emotions have not. And with Rock, my emotional and physical sides seem finally in sync. Consensual sex has to be better, right?

For the first time in my life, I feel ready to find out, to

consent, to fully want someone inside me. For the first time in my life the idea of sex is neither repulsive or merely a physical need.

I step toward him, and lightly touch his upper arm, the size of a melon. "How long do we have before the staff show up?" My fingers stroke the protruding muscle, imagining I'm stroking him somewhere else.

I sense his heart rates increasing, both in force and in speed. He wants me, too.

But he steps back. "Do you need to feed?"

"I'm not hungry." I lick my lower lip lightly. "Not for blood, anyway."

"Listen." He holds up his hands, palms forward while backing away from me. "We can't. And the staff—"

"We can be quick."

"No, we can't. Not now. Not ever."

"Is it the age difference?" I step toward him. "Because I dig older guys." I don't, or never have before. I just know I want Rock.

"Guys old enough to be your great-great-great-great grandfather?" He tries to frown, but it comes off playful.

"I'm totally into guys old enough to be my great-great-great-great-great-great grandfather." I smile to show him I'm joking, but he doesn't smile back.

"Rock—" his chest rises as I say his name "—I know you've been around longer than me, but you don't look or act old. When we met, I figured you were about thirty, which isn't all that much older than me, and I can't see why that matters anyway. Not really. Unless I'm boring to you?"

I run my hand down the front of the soft dress, wishing it was sexier. "Or maybe you're not attracted to me?"

A sound rumbles up from low in Rock's chest that proves my point.

"Acushla," he says on an exhale. "You just escaped your captors." He frowns. "You were *raped.*" His entire body shudders. "I can't—"

"But I want..." I can't articulate what I want or why. Because he's right. Wanting him, wanting him so soon after all that happened doesn't make sense, yet I do want him. I hunger for him.

"Xavier's dungeon was traumatic," I tell him. What I told Rock last night, barely scratched the surface. "But shouldn't it be up to *me* to decide whether I'm ready to move on?"

He breathes deeply, clearly fighting against what he wants. "It's not just about that..."

"Then what?" I step toward him and the sound of his pounding blood washes through me along with his scent. I reach up to lay my hand gently on his chest and one of his hearts thumps hard against my palm.

"I..." His voice is hoarse, strained. "It's been a long time for me. A very long time."

Sliding my hand over his huge pectoral muscles, I trace their shape and then brush down over his nipple. His breathing grows labored and I look up to find conflicted heat in his oceanic eyes.

I want to banish that conflict, to make him see how badly I want him, and as I gaze into his eyes, his irises seem to undulate like true ocean waves. I want to dive into them, even if it might mean drowning.

Lifting one of his hands, I place it on my torso, his fingers curving around at least half of my ribcage and spanning the distance from my waist to my armpit. Heat from his palm radiates through my chest and quickens my breath, then I slide my hand up his chest toward his neck, as far as I can reach.

It's all I can do to keep from jumping into his arms and trusting him to catch me. If he doesn't kiss me soon—

In a flash, his other hand catches the back of my neck and he captures my lips, arching me back at such a sharp angle that all my weight's in his arms. I feel a quick rush, like I'm falling, and then I feel safe, floating in his hold, swimming in his kiss.

In spite of the fast start, our kiss begins gently, tiny nibbles as we breathe into each other, exploring and tasting as anticipation builds, hard and strong, between my legs. As we continue, intense pleasure sweeps me further into an ecstatic haze. I had no idea kissing could feel like this, especially light, tender kissing, but the effect his mouth has on mine is beyond electric. Some powerful force courses hard between us, a force like magic, like fire. And I long to be burned.

Sliding my hand over his hip, I let it inch toward the front of his jeans, my fingers tingling with the anticipation of discovering his hard, thick ridge.

Growling against me, Rock deepens our kiss, his thick tongue plunging inside my mouth, and his firm but soft lips take mine with such fervor all the blood that's not already pooled between my legs rushes to my mouth, giving me the energy to kiss him back with equal ferocity. I slide my tongue against his, relishing the taste of his skin, his saliva, even as I long for his blood.

Lifting me into his arms, he crushes our bodies together and I can no longer move any part of my body except my mouth. I don't have the will to move anything beyond my lips and my tongue anyway, and even my fingers are temporarily distracted from their pursuit.

Regaining equilibrium, I try to move my thigh against his body, hoping to find the huge bulge.

"Holy shit! Get a room!" A female voice invades our private world.

Rock pulls his lips away and then presses his forehead against mine. We both pant, trying to regain the ability to breathe without being conjoined at the mouth.

The waitress from last night passes through my peripheral vision, glaring at me like I just drained and discarded someone she loves.

Rock's grip on me loosens, but he still holds me aloft. "Hey, Chelle. You're early."

"No, boss," she snaps. "I'm not."

"Lost track of the time, I guess." He smiles at me softly, then gently sets me down on my feet. As he releases me, his hands sweep over my torso and then he quickly turns to get the bucket and mop.

I sway, feeling like I did at age nine when Jordon, the boy next door, dared me to spin around fifty times with my forehead on his baseball bat. I only made it to twenty-three turns before falling to the side, and we laughed for what seemed like hours.

Laughed until my stepfather came out to see what the noise was. Instantly, it wasn't funny anymore and Jordan never played with me again.

"Get Selina a whiskey, Chelle," Rock says. "Or whatever she wants. Selina drinks on the house." Rock adjusts himself as he walks through the bar, and I grin, knowing I caused his discomfort. My insides pulse, imagining what might have happened if Chelle hadn't walked in.

He disappears into the back hall and I turn back toward the bar where Chelle's aggressively tying back her thick, unnaturally black hair, like it attacked her and the elastic is handcuffs.

"What?" she snaps when she catches me looking.

Shaking my head, slightly, I smile. Seems we'll never be friends but there's no sense making an enemy of this woman. If she wants Rock a fraction of how badly I want him, I can understand her animosity. "You've got beautiful hair."

Her chin lifts. "Thanks. You, too." Her purse and coat stashed, she rounds the end of the bar and lifts barstools down from where they sat while Rock mopped the floor.

I step over to the bar and grab one.

She holds up her hand. "I've got it."

"Okay." I back up. Clearly exchanging hair compliments didn't do much to thaw hostilities. And Rock still hasn't returned. Is he doing something to get rid of that erection, like he did last night in the shower?

It's tempting to follow him, but that would be like lobbing a grenade into this battle with Chelle, and besides, I want to continue with Rock when we have more time—lots and lots more time.

Chelle finishes setting up the stools then goes back behind the bar.

"Same as last night?" she asks.

"Same what?" I step toward her.

"Whiskey?" She holds up a bottle.

"Sure. Thank you."

She pours a few shots of the rich amber liquid into a short glass and pushes it across the bar. It stops exactly at the edge.

"Good aim." I raise the glass toward her and smile.

She rolls her eyes, then opens a lid and digs a metal scoop into a bin of ice, mixing and breaking it up.

A red heart peeks out from under the strap of her tank top.

"I like your tattoo."

"What?" She turns toward me, scowling.

"The heart. Your tattoo." I touch my shoulder.

"Oh. Yeah. It's kind of lame. Got it when I was a kid."

I wrap my fingers around my glass. "I don't think it's lame. I always wanted a tattoo. Never had the guts."

"Bullshit. You've got purple hair."

"That's less permanent." Or at least it would have been if I'd remained human. According to Rock, I'll have lavender hair forever, unable to even dye it to back to its original blond for more than a day at a time.

She ties a black apron around her hips, hiding the front of faded black jeans that are a little too tight.

"If you want one so bad, get a tattoo," she says. "What's stopping you?"

"Maybe I will." Although I know I won't. Or rather that, if I did, it wouldn't last more than a few hours. My body would heal and push out the pigments almost as quickly as the tattoo artist could inject them under my skin.

The door to the bar opens, and I spin toward it, bracing to defend myself.

The bartender walks through.

"Hey, Kev," Chelle says.

"Hey, Chelle. Hey... girl who the boss scooped out of the alley last night." An older First Nations guy, I'd guess at least forty, Kev has drooping earlobes, no doubt from spacers he wore in his youth, and they're partially hidden by an old-fashioned hat above a long dark braid that reaches far down his back.

He grins. "Still here I see?"

I grin back at him. "Looks that way."

"Overstayed her welcome," Chelle whispers under her breath as she bends below the bar.

If I were human I wouldn't have heard her snarky

remark, so I decide not to take offense at her rudeness. She didn't mean for me to hear.

"What's your name?" Kev asks.

"Selina." Was it stupid to reveal my real name? I hope not. If these two pose any danger, Rock wouldn't have left me alone with them.

"Pretty name." Kev unlocks the cash register, then grabs a bag of limes from below the counter and starts to slice them, dropping the cut pieces into a metal container.

"Have you both known Rock a long time?" I ask.

"Pretty long," Kev says at the same time that Chelle says, "Forever."

Kev grins. "I've worked here seventeen years. Rock's a good guy. Glad to see him—"

"See me what?" Rock strides into the room, steps up beside me and grins.

Longing tugs inside me. Some deep primal need wants this man in ways I don't quite understand. I need to have him sexually and emotionally and in every way he'll let me possess him.

"See you..." Kev raises his eyebrows. "Dating?"

"That's not what this is," Rock blurts, his cheeks reddening. "I'm helping Selina out. That's all."

His words stab deep inside me, and I turn toward him, but he won't look at me. Chelle, on the other hand, grins smugly.

I tell myself he didn't mean it. Dating doesn't sound like the right word, anyway, and after the kiss we just shared, I refuse to believe that he thinks there's nothing between us.

"Helping her?" Chelle says with a fair bit of snark. "So, I guess when I walked in you were helping her breathe?"

"Yup." Rock turns toward me and winks. "That's exactly what I was doing."

CHAPTER TEN

Selina

Rock gets up to deal with a liquor vendor, leaving me in the back booth of his bar where I have a good view of the door. Rock and I have been chatting for the past few hours, getting to know each other better, and the more I know him the more I like him. At first glance, he might look like a tough guy—literally a Viking come out of time to rape and pillage...but that couldn't be further from the reality of Rock.

I sense he has darkness in his past, but instead of turning toward it, he's chosen to be kind, to care about other people, and now he's asked his vampire friends to help me, too.

I love the way he asks questions gently, then listens to me with such deep intent. I've barely known him twenty-four hours and I've already shown him more of myself than I've shown anyone.

I'm tempted to head back to the alley where Rock went

to meet with the vendor, or maybe they're already carrying boxes downstairs. I could help.

But before I can move, the door opens, and Rock's vampire friends are obvious to spot.

The male vampire, Malcolm, is average in height with an olive complexion and curly jet-black hair. His most striking feature is his mouth, his lips red and plump, almost like he's wearing lipstick although his lips are bare. His mate, Astrid, is nearly as tall, with voluptuous curves and flowing red hair framing a pale complexion.

They're well dressed but nothing too showy, and although they stand out to me, they fit right in at Rock's bar filled with a mixture of artsy types, hipsters and a few full-on alcoholics.

Nothing specific marks Rock's friends as vampires, but to my eyes, it's like they glow from the inside. Malcolm and his mate are beautiful to me in a way that I can't quite describe, but I've noticed in all vampires—even Pike.

My hand trembles as I raise my glass of whiskey, hoping to take one last sip, but only a few drops ring the bottom of the glass. I wish I had more, if for no other reason than for something to do with my hands, but no way am I asking Chelle to get me another.

The waitress glares at me with a look she clearly wishes could kill as she heads to another table with a tray full of bottles and glasses. I rise, planning to ask Kev to pour me a drink, but Astrid turns around, spots me and smiles.

She looks even more beautiful when smiling, like rainbows are flowing from her eyes, and I can't understand why everyone in the bar isn't staring. She touches Malcolm's shoulder. He nods, then turns back to Kev as the female walks toward me.

"Hi." She slides into the booth opposite me. "You must be Selina. I'm Astrid."

Everything inside me freezes. I know she's Rock's friend and I know that Rock wouldn't do anything to put me in danger, but somehow my brain can't convince the adrenaline that's coursing through me. My fight-or-flight instincts are on high.

"Don't worry, Selina. I'm a friend. Rock's friend. Your friend soon, too, I hope." She smiles again and her radiance melts into my apprehension. Is she controlling my mind?

"No, Selina. Vampires can't do that. Or, rather, if some can it's extremely rare."

"But you can read minds! You knew what I was thinking."

Her laugh has musical tones. "What? No. Ha! You asked if I was controlling your mind."

"I said that out loud?" I laugh in embarrassment.

"Did you really think I might be able to do that?" She shakes her head. "Rock said you were a baby, but I had no idea how little you know."

Hurt constricts my chest. "Rock called me a baby?"

"A baby *vamp*." She stretches her hand across the table toward me. "Newly turned. In vampire culture, baby isn't an insult."

Malcolm approaches and sets three drinks on the table. "Astrid, are you insulting our new friend so soon?" He pushes what looks like a triple whiskey toward me. "Slide down," he says to his mate and then sits beside her.

"Hi, Selina," he says. "I'm Malcolm. Rock told us a little about you. I hope we can help."

"Hi." I shake his hand as he wraps the other arm around his mate.

She snuggles in tight beside him and sips on her drink,

some kind of sophisticated-looking cocktail, which suits her. I can smell orange and something bitter mixed in with the whiskey. Malcolm's drink is clear and—I inhale—it's gin with something even more herbal mixed in. I'm still discovering the bounds of my ability to sense things around me.

"Rock says someone's hunting you?" he says.

Fear shoots through me again, but before I can fully process my emotion, or Malcolm's question, Rock arrives, sliding into the booth beside me. His weight makes the wood dip and his warmth gives me strength.

"You can trust Malcolm and Astrid." He drapes his arm around me. "I didn't tell them much. It's your story to tell."

I nod, then take a sip of whiskey for courage. Alcohol doesn't make me inebriated, but still takes the edge off. The whiskey relaxes me, even if the effect wears off within minutes.

"Have you heard of King Xavier?" I ask.

Astrid's face blanches and Malcolm frowns. "We know of him," he says darkly. "He formed some fake royal court, far before the true king died."

"The true king?" I ask.

"Your Maker taught you nothing?" Malcolm asks with dismay.

I shake my head.

"Well then, we'd better start at the beginning. Tell me everything you remember about your transition."

I recount the part of the story I told Rock, and when I describe my Maker, Malcolm and Astrid share a quick glance.

"Do you guys know her?" Rock asks them. "Selina's Maker?"

Astrid shakes her head. "No. But based on your description, she could be a vampire the security team at FJS have questioned before."

"FJS?"

"It's where we work," Malcolm says.

"A vampire syndicate," Rock adds.

"I keep telling you." Astrid wags her finger at Rock. "FJS is not a syndicate. We're not like the syndicates, at all."

Rock shrugs. "Walks like a duck..."

"We can get into FJS later," Malcolm says. "Right now, just know that we can help keep you safe. Some vamp has been killing humans all over Toronto. It's put the police on high alert. They've set up traps."

My eyes open wide. "I nearly got caught in a police trap last night. If Rock hadn't been there..." I lean against him and he bends to kiss the top of my head.

"We can get you a place to live in a corporate residence," Malcolm says. "We'll vouch for you." He smiles at his spouse.

I shake my head. "No. That is—" I turn to Rock.

"You're welcome to stay with me as long as you want." He squeezes my shoulder.

"I want to stay with Rock. For now, at least." The words fill me with happiness.

"Staying here is safer than a *lot* of places." Astrid takes a sip of her drink. "But there are some logistics to work out. Like, when's the last time you fed?"

"Last night," I answer.

"But she was starved for over a year before that," Rock adds. "She was weak when I found her, even though she'd just fed."

"We'll take you to FJS," she says. "You can feed safely there."

"From blood slaves?" I know how the syndicates feed,

how the vampires in Xavier's court did. I shudder and I'm sure my disdain is clear.

"Slaves?" Astrid looks offended. "All FJS employees—vampire and human—are *paid* for their services. And yes, some of the humans provide blood for vampires, but they do so willingly and they're very well compensated."

I frown. "But the venom keeps them from remembering. That doesn't sound consensual to me."

"How is it consensual when you feed on the street?" Malcolm asks.

It seems different, but I can't explain why. My concept of a blood slave is likely colored by the human media, but I find it extremely distasteful. Immoral.

Astrid holds up her hand. "Fine. You don't like the idea of using our staff, but you can't feed off some random human in an alley. It's dangerous, and you never know what quality you're going to get."

I raise my chin. "I did just fine on my own. At least until..." I look down. In spite of my claim, I was a mess on my own. Nearly sunburned or caught by the police so many times. And then I made the mistake of going with Santos. I want to be someone who can take care of herself but have to face facts.

Astrid reaches over the table toward me. "When's the last time you fed from a vampire?"

I shake my head.

I've never fed from a vampire, although I suppose I can't quite be sure that all the sips of blood I had in the dungeon came from humans. Tasted human to me.

"The club?" Astrid shoots a look toward her mate, and he raises a shoulder in what looks like agreement. She turns back to me. "We'll take you somewhere you can feed safely."

"Can you come, too?" I whisper to Rock. The idea of leaving his side seems unthinkable.

He looks across to his friends. "I don't think so, Acushla."

"Where we're taking you," Astrid says. "It's vampires only."

"But...if it's vampires only, how will I feed?" My nose wrinkles. Blood slaves in a club are no better than blood slaves in an office.

"From a vampire," she answers like it's obvious. "If you were still weak after feeding last night, I suspect that's what you need."

"Really? Without being their mate?" Xavier and his guards fed on me, but I assumed that was part of my torture, not for their nourishment. I've only seen vampires feeding off each other as part of marriage ceremonies, and as part of the description of sex between mates that Xavier described in lurid detail when he was trying to woo me.

"Are you claiming you've never fed from a vampire?" Astrid asks.

I nod. "Never."

The shock on Astrid's face is obvious. "Not since your Maker?"

"I didn't feed from my Maker, either."

"But you must have," Astrid says. "Or you wouldn't have transitioned. It's not possible."

"So I've heard." I shrug. "I don't know what to tell you, but I didn't feed from the vampire the night I turned. I remember everything about that night so clearly. Too clearly." I shudder.

"Then you'd better finish telling the story," Malcolm says.

I draw a deep breath. I've been holding in my story for

so long it's formed a hard, painful lump in my chest. Perhaps it is time to share it—especially with vampires who might be able to make sense of what happened.

The other three sit patiently, waiting for me to begin, and I take another long sip of whiskey for courage.

"She punctured my neck, and I felt the powerful suction of her thirst." The memory shivers through me. "She drained me, completely, then she dropped me to the asphalt. I was barely conscious but knew I was going to die. Maybe I did die." I shake my head. "I don't understand what happened, but I remember every moment of it."

Rock squeezes my shoulders, pulling me against him.

"It was eleven forty one when she left me to die."

"How are you so sure of the time?" Astrid's eyes narrow. "You shouldn't remember *any* of this."

"Always the investigator." Malcolm nudges her.

"I know the time," I reply, "because I could see the reflection of a clock in a puddle." I can still see the image, the red and yellow logo for Citywide Donuts, and below that a blue digital display with the time and temperature.

"As I lay there, I watched the time change in the puddle," I tell them. "Every minute I felt physically weaker, but more determined to live."

"A half hour passed, and I still couldn't move."

I lay there, my right arm extended on the pavement, watching the puddle as the clock turned to twelve seventeen. The skin on my arm was so white, almost translucent, and while I could see my arm, I couldn't feel it. Not in a normal way. But I hadn't survived my stepfather's abuse to die that night. Not like that. I was starting my dream job the next day. Lark and I planned to get a real apartment together. I had an entire life ahead of me, and I refused to die at twenty-two.

"I concentrated on my arm," I tell them, "and it started to tingle. Time passed and soon my entire body was tingling."

Tingle is the only word I have to describe the sensation, because in some ways it was similar to how it feels when you rub life back into an arm that's asleep, and yet it was different.

"The tingle was intensely painful," I tell them, "like my body was being pierced by a million shards of glass, like my veins were filled with acid. But at least I was feeling something."

Malcolm nods. "Transitions can be rough. Your Maker should have offered her blood to you, long before it got to that."

"Well, she was gone, and the pain intensified. It was like I was dying, but at the same time I sensed life flowing back into my body."

Astrid nods some encouragement. "What else?"

"I screamed, I think, but people passing by the end of the alley didn't react or stop, so I guess my screams weren't audible."

I sink back into my thoughts as I remember that nightmare of a night. Concentrating on my index finger I watched it until finally it moved, lifting just a few millimeters from the damp pavement. But when it dropped again, a fresh rush of pain raced through me like fire. The pain was unbearable. But I had to bear it. I had to bear it to survive.

"Time passed," I say aloud, "and I challenged myself to move, even though it brought pain. Every minute I moved another part of my body, working through my fingers and toes, then moving on to a hand, then a foot."

"Finally, at one fifty-two, I slid my entire forearm along the pavement. The pain was so strong it turned my vision white. I was sure I was dying, seeing the flash of light before death. But the flash faded, or maybe I got used to the pain, along with the acid that had replaced my bloodstream."

The truth is, the pain became part of me, joining forces with the emotional pain I'd carried most of my life, but I don't tell them that part. It's too personal. Too horrible.

Closing my eyes, I remember how memories of my childhood abuse flashed through my mind that night, replaying vividly as if it were happening again, as if the horrors were staking out their place in my new state of being, implanting themselves in the new version of me so that I'd never be able to escape.

I know where I am right now—in Rock's bar. I can feel his arm around me, smell the whiskey and beer, but my mind is in two other places as well, in that alley *and* in my childhood bedroom. The memories are vivid, too vivid.

I squash down the memories of my childhood, but that night I used the pain from the abuse to power my body. I used my agony as fuel.

The strength I'd found to say no to my stepfather—again and again—to push him off me, to finally leave that house, gave me the strength to push through the pain of transition and get up off that alleyway asphalt.

Forcing my mind back into the bar, I open my eyes and wait to catch my breath. How do I explain this part of the memory to the others? The way I used my childhood pain to get me through that night in the alley.

There's no way I'm telling Astrid and Malcolm the details of that part, not even Rock. I don't want anyone to know what my stepfather did to me.

"I concentrated," I tell them. "I used all my strength and emotions to give me the power to push off that alley pavement. I was weak, my blood and mind were on fire, but I was alive and I was moving. Then I heard a sound in the alley. A voice."

It felt like the voice was coming from another dimension, but I don't dare tell them the details of this part, either, because I recognized the voice. And it called out my name.

"A figure crouched beside me," I say aloud, "a woman, and I felt an overpowering need for her blood. Her body coursed with a river of something I wanted, something I instinctively knew I needed to survive. The scent—coppery, sweet, so alive—overpowered every other thought inside me and every sense except the pain. The pain remained."

Malcolm nods and sets down his glass. "Please, continue."

"The woman's blood overtook my thoughts... " All I had left in my mind was her blood and my pain. And the pain turned into a force that shouted for me to claim what I needed, to consume what this woman's body had on offer so I could survive.

"I pounced on her," I say aloud, shuddering at the vivid memory. "One second I was belly down on the asphalt, and the next I was on top of the woman, pinning her down. My teeth plunged into her throat, and I drank."

I drank and drank and drank. The hot elixir stored in her body soothed my pain and built inside me a new sense of power, of life. A new sense of existence.

"My vision turned bright red as I fed," I tell them. But I did more than feed. I pulled forth every drop I could find.

When her body had no more to give, I lifted my head and sucked in a long sharp breath.

"After," I continue aloud, "I could taste the molecules of air, sense *everything*. It was like I could differentiate every little thing that the passing air had contacted before it reached me."

"I know exactly what you mean," Astrid says softly. "I had that same feeling the first time I fed."

Closing my eyes, I nod, glad to tell this story to someone who understands. Overcome by the world, I covered my ears, closed my eyes and tried not to breathe all the strong smells. But eventually, I let the sounds and smells and sights of my environment sink in.

I could see individual grains of clay in the brick walls, smell individual bacterium swimming in the murky puddles, and the lights... My night vision kicked in for the first time, and it was hard to keep my eyes fully open.

Opening my eyes now, I see that the three of them are waiting for me to continue.

"A couple passed by the end of the alley," I say, "and my vision was so clear that I saw a tiny cross tattoo on the woman's inner wrist. I could smell a shit stain on the man's underwear and hear their individual heartbeats." I shake my head. The details are vivid, but they don't matter.

"I didn't fully understand what was happening. I knew vampires existed but had very little knowledge beyond a few stories I'd read online. I knew I'd just drank blood, but none of it made sense to me."

"How did you figure it out?" Rock asks.

Looking down at my hands, I shake my head. "I don't know. It just fell into place, I guess."

I can't share the next part. Not ever. That night, feeling powerful but scared, I looked down and saw the truth—the awful truth. The woman I'd fed from was dead.

I staggered back from the murder scene, the murder I'd committed. Another kind of pain invaded my mind that night, one even worse than the physical pain.

I'd killed her. I'd killed my one and only friend.

My friend Lark was dead, her face in a puddle, her neck pierced by my fangs, but the wound barely bled. She had no more blood to lose.

I'd killed Lark to survive, but if I could have reversed what I'd done, if I could have taken all her blood from inside me and put it back where it belonged, I would have done it, even if it meant my own death.

That night, turning away from my friend's lifeless body, I ran. I ran like a coward. A murderer. A monster.

CHAPTER ELEVEN

Rock

I hug Selina's shaking body against my side. Pain is etched into every part of her. Her retelling was so vivid I feel sure her mind was transported back to that night as she told the story, that her body re-experienced the trauma as we sat here in the booth.

Even before hearing her story I knew that she'd suffered, but to hear details of her agonizing transformation, her guilt at killing her first source of blood...

She'd never admitted that last part, not directly, but the truth was clear in her expression.

That kind of guilt I know well, and my hearts ache knowing she went through so much, knowing she'll be suffering the trauma of killing that human for the rest of her life, the rest of eternity. Time hasn't dented my pain.

I want to take Selina downstairs where I can hold her and kiss her, help her forget, but the two vampires sitting at our booth are right. She needs to feed.

Mostly quiet as Selina told her story, Astrid frowns now.

"Spontaneous transformation." Malcolm shakes his head. "I thought it was a myth."

"It is a myth." Astrid shakes her head. "There's no way. Unless..." She leans toward Selina. "Who are your parents?"

Selina swipes her hand across her cheekbone like she thought there were tears there. "My mom...she was..." Selina fights to form words.

"Was?" Astrid asks bluntly. "Your mother is dead?"

"No." Selina draws a ragged breath. "At least I'm not sure. I haven't tried to see her since my transition."

"When did you last see her?" asks Astrid.

"I ran away from home when I was fourteen," Selina says softly.

"How come?" Malcolm asks and I want to kick him. The way Selina's body reacts to the question, almost caving in on itself, gives a strong hint at the answer.

"My stepfather was a jerk," Selina says. "I couldn't stay in that house." She shakes her head. "I never talked to my mom after I left, but I checked in on her. I'd watch her come and go. Make sure that my stepfather hadn't killed her."

"He hit her?" Malcolm asks. "Why didn't you or your mom report your stepfather to the cops?"

Astrid slaps his arm and shoots him a look to tell him his question was insensitive.

"I didn't want the cops to know I was living on the streets," Selina answers. "I didn't trust adults, and I figured I was better off on my own."

"What about your real father?" Malcolm asks. "Who was he?"

Selina shakes her head. "I never met him. He was a one-night stand. Mom never told him she was pregnant. To be honest, I'm not positive she knew who my father was."

"So, after you turned," Astrid says. "How did you survive alone?"

Selina's hand trembles and she cups her glass. She takes a sip of her whiskey, and I signal Chelle to bring us another round.

"For the first month or so," Selina says, "I hid in the boiler room of the scuzzy rooming house where I'd been living. I only went out when I was desperate to feed. But the owner found me and threatened to call the cops because of unpaid rent. Luckily, he didn't recognize *what* I was, but it was clear I could never go back there."

I rub her arm, wishing I could pulverize her pain.

"Then what?" Malcolm asks.

"I went from place to place looking for shelter from the sun. I think the longest I spent in one location was five days. It was hard."

"Why didn't you join a syndicate?" Astrid prods. "And how the hell did you end up with a scumbag like Xavier?"

"Give her time." Malcolm kisses her cheek.

Selina draws a long breath before speaking again. "Every time I found shelter, a syndicate recruiter would find me within a couple of nights. And, no offense," she glances across the table, "but the syndicate recruiters creeped me out—all threats wrapped in promises of safety."

Malcolm snorts.

Selina lifts her chin in defiance. "All I knew about vampire syndicates was what I'd heard in the news. I thought they were crime gangs that bribed police and politicians and..." She sucks in a breath. "Captured humans to use as blood slaves."

"All bullshit," Malcolm says.

"Some of it's not bullshit." Astrid frowns at her mate, then turns to Selina. "Not every syndicate is like that, though. Yes, syndicates do strike deals with the police in exchange for protection, but it's not all crime and corruption."

Astrid looks around the room. "I'm starting to worry we might be overheard."

"You're safe in my bar," I assure them.

"Rock, with all due respect," Astrid says, "you don't know that. I love that you've made a safe place for us here, but you can't control who comes in."

"Let's go downstairs." I should have taken us down as soon as Malcolm and Astrid got here. Selina's the only person who's ever been in my apartment, but right now I'll do anything to keep her safe.

"No." Astrid shakes her head. "Selina needs to come with us, so she can feed."

I want Selina to get everything she needs and I trust my friends, but the idea of leaving her side, for even a minute, hurts deep in my heart.

CHAPTER TWELVE

Selina

I've only been with Rock for twenty-four hours, but sitting here, sheltered by his huge, warm body and our thighs pressed together, the idea of leaving his side seems wrong. So does leaving the bar—going out in the open where Pike might find me.

But with every passing moment, I'm even more hungry.

A woman in red jeans passes our table and the scent of her blood pulls me up a few inches from my seat. Without Rock's arm around me, I might have followed her to take what I need.

No way can I put Rock at risk by feeding on one of his customers. Plus, Astrid and Malcolm claim what I need is vampire blood.

I look at the two vampires across from us. "If I need to feed from a vampire..." I clear my throat. "Can't I just feed from one of you?"

Malcolm looks ill. Shock flashes on Astrid's face but

quickly disappears. "Honey. We're a committed couple. We never give our vein to another vampire."

"Oh. Sorry." I have so much to learn about vampire science and culture.

"You still didn't tell us how you ended up with Xavier," Astrid says. "I'm sorry, but before we invite you to the club, I need to know more."

"That's okay," I say. "I can understand why you're skeptical. I wish I'd been more skeptical."

"How's that?" Astrid asks.

"Well, I told you how I was approached, practically stalked, by syndicate recruiters?"

She nods. "It's possible you even met someone from FJS. We have an outreach program targeting strays."

"Strays?"

She looks apologetic, but she's right. I was a stray and I supposed I've always been a stray—first as a human, then a vampire. But if being a stray was tough for a human, it was worse as a vampire. Literally every human on Earth was out to kill me.

"One night," I tell them, "I met a vampire, Santos, who seemed different from the others—well-dressed, sophisticated, a Spanish accent. He chased away another recruiter who was threatening to turn me in to the cops if I didn't join his syndicate."

"Asshole," Malcolm says. "No one from FJS would ever do that."

I shiver, remembering the bullying nature of the recruiter Santos sent away, how the vampire claimed I was violating codes I didn't know existed: feeding in public without authorization, sleeping in unsanctioned locations, risking the reputation of all vampire-kind.

I was scared and guilty and so alone.

"Santos told me he lived under the protection of a great king." I swallow a lump in my throat. "I didn't know vampires had royalty and was fascinated by the idea. Plus a royal court seemed way more legit than a syndicate."

"Not at all legit." Malcolm says the last word with scorn. "There is one true king.

"At least there *was* a true king," Astrid interjects. "He's been missing for twenty years."

"What happened to him?" I ask.

"No one knows." Malcolm's eyes fill with sadness. "And in his absence, the syndicates and these bogus royal courts gained power. It's the same all over the world. Chaos."

I soak in this knowledge about my species, thirsting for more, but that's not all I'm thirsting for.

"FJS is different, though," Astrid adds. "Our corporation has been around for centuries. Plus, we were sanctioned by the monarchy."

"That's why we get offended when you compare us to a syndicate." Malcolm points at Rock.

"Fair enough," Rock says.

"What does FJS stand for?" I ask.

"*Fides, Juris, Sanctorum,*" Malcolm answers. "Latin words loosely meaning loyalty, justice and the sacred. But no one uses the full name."

"So." Astrid taps the table. "Santos? You didn't finish your story."

"Yeah." I draw a breath. "Santos painted this picture of a safe and loving community where I'd never again have to hunt for my meals or a place to hide from the sunlight. It sounded too good to be true, even better than what the syndicates were promising." I shake my head. "I was so tired. So alone."

"Baby girl." Astrid squeezes my hand. "I get it. In the same situation I might have followed him, too."

I smile at her, starting to truly like Rock's friends.

"But how long were you with Xavier?" Astrid leans forward. "How can I be sure you're not *still* with him?"

"She's not," Rock interjects. "Bastard raped her. Tortured her."

"Oh, I'm so sorry." Astrid stands and reaches across the table toward me. I rise, too, and she hugs me, rubbing my back.

I sit down and take a sip of my whiskey. "Santos presented me to Xavier like some kind of bounty, and the king took a liking to me."

"Again," Malcolm interjects, "not a king."

"I know that *now*." I tip my head to the side. "I guess I was a little flattered by the king's attention at first. Everyone made such a big deal about it. And life at his court *was* safe and easier than my life on the streets, and... and... it was sexy." I twist my lips to the side, embarrassed at how easily I was seduced. "But then everything changed, or at least I started to see things more clearly." I shake my head.

"Tell us more," Astrid prompts.

"I didn't have any freedom. Xavier's Guard watched me, night and day. Supposedly, it was for my protection as the king's future mate, but soon I realized I was his prisoner and he was determined to marry me, whether I wanted to or not."

I tell them about my failed marriage ceremonies and some of what followed. I leave out the worst parts, but at each detail I give, Rock's hold on me tightens. His body tenses like actual rock, and I know if he ever met Xavier, he'd kill him—if the powerful vampire didn't kill Rock first.

Chelle arrives at the table and sets down another round of drinks.

"Thanks, Chelle," Rock says.

"No sweat, boss." She smiles at him, then shoots me a sneer. "Shall I keep them coming?"

"Actually," he says. "My friends are going to take off."

"Great!" she says with way too much enthusiasm.

"And I'm going with them." He looks over at Malcolm and Astrid. "I could use a walk."

Chelle walks away, muttering under her breath, "Fucking vamps."

My belly tightens and I lean toward Malcolm and Astrid. "Did you hear that?"

"Hear what?" Rock asks.

"Chelle knows we're vampires," I whisper to him. "Or that Malcolm and Astrid are, anyway." My heart rate triples. Chelle already hates me. If she calls the police...

"It's okay," Rock says. "Chelle and Kev have been with me for years. You're all safe here. I promise."

I glance toward Chelle, just as she looks back toward me. The hatred in her eyes...

I guess I understand. I'd be jealous, if she were the one with Rock. I resolve to be extra nice to her, make it extra hard for her to hate me.

"Well, Selina," Astrid downs her drink. "I guess that's our cue to exit. We have to get you fed and back before dawn."

CHAPTER THIRTEEN

Selina

Astrid and Malcolm's limo lets us out in front of a typical-looking east-end bungalow, one of hundreds of nearly identical homes built in the middle of the last century.

"This is as far as I go." Rock bends to kiss me softly, then he holds me and whispers, "I'll see you soon, Acushla. Get what you need. And remember I will be here waiting for you, no matter what happens."

"What do you think might happen?"

"Nothing in particular." He smiles, but there's a hint of regret in his eyes. "Just remember I'm here for you. Now go." He releases me from his hold.

I reluctantly follow Malcolm and Astrid through a totally normal looking garden gate and down a paved path to the bungalow's porch. I turn back at the door.

Rock moves into the shadows of a large maple tree and leans back against its trunk. No human will be able to spot him there unless they shine a light directly toward the tree.

Malcolm types a code into a lock, then pulls open the door. “Ladies.” He sweeps out his arm. “After you.”

I step into the generic-looking home, everything in grays and whites with chrome accents and graphic stylized portraits of old movie stars. It looks like the place was decorated at least a couple of decades ago.

“This way.” Astrid beckons for me to follow and she leads me past the basement stairs to the kitchen.

She presses a tiny gold button in the middle of the refrigerator door, one so small I doubt a human eye could detect it, and then tugs open the fridge. The fridge shelves and their sparse contents slide back to reveal a staircase leading down into darkness.

Behind Astrid, I descend the stairs to a long hallway, the floor a dark slate and the walls upholstered with black satin punctuated by nails or pins that reflect the light as if each head is a gem. Perhaps they are.

Astrid opens a door at the top of another long staircase leading down. My stomach tightens. This is too much like going down into Xavier’s dungeon.

I grab her shoulder. “I thought you said this was a club? Where is everyone?”

Turning back, she smiles and takes my hand. “They’re all another two flights down. The club is deep so no vibrations from the music carry up to any of the neighborhood homes.”

Vibrations—or screams?

I will myself to be brave. If this vampire couple has nefarious plans, it’s already too late. Rock can’t hear me from down here and there’s no way I can fight them off myself.

I continue to follow Astrid, and as we go down farther the sound of pumping bass vibrates up through my feet and then into my ears. Astrid opens the fourth door we encounter, and music bursts out like it had been caged.

Behind the door, lights flash to illuminate red satin walls, not to mention our clothes and skin, as we descend yet another flight of stairs. At the end of a short hall at the bottom, a huge, tuxedo-wearing vampire stands, arms crossed over his chest.

"Hey, Jordie," Astrid says. "This is Selina. She's with us."

"Nice," Jordie says as he looks me up and down. He winks at Malcolm. "You two taking a second mate?"

I cringe. Is that what this is?

"No," Malcolm says. "Selina's just a friend."

The word *friend* warms something inside me. Other than Lark, I've never really had friends. When I was a kid, I didn't dare bring anyone home to face the monster, and he refused to let me go to the few playdates I requested before giving up.

The steel door Jordie's guarding is massive and dancing with light. "Are those crystals?" I whisper in Astrid's ear.

"Diamonds," Jordie says with a huff, clearly insulted.

Who owns this club? I wonder, as Jordie swings open the door.

We step into the room, and sounds and sights and scents bombard me. It's the most beautiful space I've ever seen—and that includes Xavier's decadent palace, which was more garish than beautiful.

The walls and ceiling sparkle as thousands of lights dance over what must be more diamonds. Even the floor seems to glow. The music is contemporary, similar to what I've heard passing bars in the human world, and just loud enough to fill the room and still allow conversation.

A bar stretches along the side of the room, and bottles behind it glimmer under lights. The bar itself is made of glass, etched in beautiful patterns that seem to shift as the bartenders serve drinks from behind it.

I'm underdressed in my gray jersey dress and Keds, and even Astrid's gorgeous sheer blouse and form-fitting leather pants seem conservative here. But no one stares or makes us feel uncomfortable.

"Let's get a drink." Astrid, still holding my hand, pulls me toward the bar. Malcolm heads the other direction, clearly spotting someone he knows.

"Whiskey?" Astrid asks as she leans against the glass structure.

I shake my head. "I don't have any money."

"Don't worry about it." She smiles at the Asian bartender when he approaches. The vampire is tall and bare chested, his body sculpted and hairless, and the blood pounding through his veins smells so delicious I want to vault over the top of the bar and dig in my fangs.

"Who's the baby?" he asks.

"Am I that obvious?" My cheeks heat.

"No need to be embarrassed." He leans toward us. "We don't get many babies in here. She yours?" he asks Astrid.

She shakes her head. "I'll have a Sazerac, a double, and my friend here—"

"I'll have the same," I interrupt. I love my straight-up whiskey, but it's a night for new things and whatever Astrid was drinking earlier smelled delicious. I trust her taste.

As the bartender makes our drinks, Astrid and I lean back against the bar, looking out at the club. The area immediately in front of us is filled with small high-top tables and dozens of vampires talking and sipping on cocktails. Beyond that lies a dance floor. It's hard to be sure, but the dance floor looks like glass, too. Past that, I can barely make out what looks like a lounge area in the distance.

"This place is huge," I say.

"It's under the entire block," Astrid replies. "Plus the next one over. Humans have no idea."

"How long has it been here? Who owns it?"

"It's owned by FJS, the company Malc and I work for, and it was built at the same time as the houses, although it's been upgraded over the years."

"How does everyone get in here without humans noticing?" There are hundreds of vamps down here, maybe a thousand, and if they all come and go through that house on any given night, I can't believe the place hasn't been raided.

"There are several ways in," Astrid says.

"Here you go, ladies." The bartender sets down our drinks.

I pick up my glass and twist it around, loving how the light dances through both the vessel and its contents. Down here, everything seems like a work of art.

Taking a sip of the drink, I close my eyes in pleasure. "Wow, that's delicious." It's like the best whiskey I've ever had, but with sweet and bitter notes added in. A thin section of orange peel swims in the amber yumminess and adds just the right hint of citrus.

"Glad you like it. See anything else down here you like?" Astrid nudges me. "Does anything beyond the drink smell delicious? I mean, *anyone*?"

I grin, my cheeks on fire. Ever since I got down here I've been hungry for vampire blood. Something I never really knew I wanted, and it's a good time to ask Astrid questions.

"I've never felt a hunger for vampire blood." As I say the words, I realize I'm lying. I *have* felt it before. Once before. But the memory of yearning for Pike's blood chills the warmth I've been feeling, so I try to forget it. "How come I feel it so strongly tonight?"

"You're a bit of a mystery." Astrid takes a sip of her drink. "Until you're fully formed, you should only crave your Maker's blood. Thirsting for another vamp's blood doesn't typically start for a couple of decades."

"Does that mean...could my Maker be down here? Is that why I'm so thirsty?"

She shakes her head. "I doubt it. Everyone down here either works for FJS or has been carefully vetted. You wouldn't have gotten in so easily if you weren't with me." She sets her cocktail down on the shiny bar. "I'm head of security."

Glancing around the chatting patrons, it's like I can smell each and every one of them, both separately and together. The scent is so strong it makes me weak in the knees and, I notice with some horror, wet between the legs.

"What's happening to me?"

Astrid strokes my upper arm. "You're growing up." She raises her eyebrows a few times. "You're so different from most babies so it's hard to be sure, but I guess you weren't ready to feel this craving before tonight. And your story about being made—"

"It's not a story. That's what happened."

She hides her obvious skepticism behind her glass as she takes another sip of her cocktail.

"How do I choose?" I glance around the room. The females smell as delicious as the males, and as my hunger builds, I want to taste everyone. "Do I get to choose?"

"Well..." Astrid lays her hand on my arm. "Malcolm and I talked on the way over, and we have an idea."

"I don't get any say?"

"Sure you do." She rubs my arm. "If you don't like him,

that's okay. We'll find someone else. But feeding, it's a very —a very *intimate* act. I can't really describe it. Malc and I want to make sure that you're going to be safe."

"Safe?" My heart starts pounding.

"No one here would hurt you," she says. "There's no need to be afraid of that, but just like humans, some vampires are rougher than others, and some more possessive. And I know you like Rock."

"It's that obvious?"

"Honey..." She laughs. "That's why we don't want your first time to be with someone who might want to *claim* you."

"Claim me?"

"Take you away from Rock."

"That's not going to happen." After my experience with Xavier, I will never let myself be *claimed* again.

She shrugs in a way that says it might not be my choice. "Selina, when you feed tonight...you might want to claim the vampire you feed from, too."

"What?"

"If you're compatible, the feeding might bring on... certain intimate feelings. So we think you should feed from someone who won't reciprocate any feelings that may arise inside you."

"Okay." She's crazy if she thinks I'm going to have *intimate* feelings about anyone other than Rock. But I guess I should be thankful that she's taking precautions.

"The vampire we have in mind is a friend," Astrid says. "He'll stay detached. Just let you feed without..."

"Without what?"

She smiles. "Let's just say you'll never get a marriage proposal from this guy."

This is starting to feel more like Xavier's court and I don't like that.

"Why mention marriage proposals? Didn't you say that vampires don't have to be mates to feed from each other?"

She nods. "Yes. But feeding between vampires is intimate. As intimate as sex."

I suck in a sharp breath. In spite of my reluctance to be here, my intense thirst continues to build, and it's a hunger for more than just blood. I don't want to have sex with anyone but Rock, but my entire body pulses with need.

Scanning the crowd, I eye a slender but sculpted, dark-skinned vampire. He moves like a track and field star as he approaches a slightly effeminate male wearing a pink silk jumpsuit. The two couldn't be more opposite to each other, but right now I want them both—their blood, anyway. I'm losing my mind.

"Which one is your friend?" I ask, my voice slightly breathless.

"Malcolm is looking for him. He'll tell him what we need. What *you* need."

Anticipation dances inside me. I was desperate for human blood last night, so hungry and weak, but my need for vampire blood is even stronger. More than a matter of survival.

"While we're waiting..." Astrid puts down her drink "... how about we dance."

I set down my drink and follow my new friend through the groups of chatting vampires. As we get closer to the dance floor, the volume of the music increases until I can feel my eardrums move.

We join the gyrating dancers. I look down and gasp. The floor is glass, as I suspected, and there's a pool underneath. Several vampires are swimming beneath us, totally naked.

"How do they breathe?" I whisper in Astrid's ear.

"You haven't tried swimming yet?" she asks, but doesn't wait for an answer. "Most vampires can stay under water a half hour or more without coming up for air."

I had no idea. A female vampire swims up below me, smiling, her dark hair swirling around her like a deep-sea creature, then a male swims up from below her, his skin pale against her brown complexion and his erection obvious.

He grabs her from behind, and I gasp.

I crouch down as if I can reach through the glass to protect her, but she doesn't fight him, and within moments, their bodies are joined. He holds her hips tightly as he drives into her from behind, and she braces on the glass between us.

The act is too intimate to be on display, but I can't look away, and the need between my legs intensifies.

Astrid pulls me up from my crouch, a knowing grin on her face. "Come on. We came out here to dance."

She moves, her hips swaying and the rest of her flowing along in perfect time to the music. I've never been much of a dancer, but caught up in Astrid's motion and the energy of the others around me, I'm swept into the current of movement. My awkwardness vanishes.

I can't remember ever having this much fun.

CHAPTER FOURTEEN

Grayson

Watching the dance floor below, I lean back against the pillar, absentmindedly playing with one of Kara's tits. The slender vamp is nearly as tall as me—and she's sexy as shit—but I'm bored.

Or not in the mood.

Odd, because I'm always in the mood.

"Earth to Grayson." Kara's hand brushes my cock.

"That's nice, luv." I glance at her and smile. "Just like that."

"Nice?" Through the trousers of one of my best bespoke suits, she squeezes me hard, and I'm fully stiff within seconds.

My cock's in the game, but my mind still isn't.

Kara reaches up to loosen my tie, probably planning to go for my jugular, but I grab her hand. "Later?"

"What's wrong?" she asks, straightening her red silk

gown, pulling it back up over the tit I barely noticed exposing.

Kara's objectively gorgeous—I'm sure she turned heads even before her transition—and normally I enjoy her as a sexual partner, but I'm not into it tonight.

She grabs my package again, clearly hoping I'll change my mind.

I sigh. I could give her a quick fuck, seems like the polite thing to do, but all this random shagging is getting old. I shouldn't have come to the club tonight. I'm going to head home.

"Nothing's wrong, pet." I grab her wrist. "I'm just distracted. Can we get together later? Find me before dawn?"

"Sure." Her smile quickly turns aloof. "That is, if *I'm* still in the mood." She kisses my cheek.

Kara sashays away, making sure I take note of how juicy her arse looks in the tight red packaging of that dress. My stiffy stirs, but going home is still the most appealing option.

Getting ready to leave, I spot Astrid on the dance floor below. She's mated to my dear friend Malcolm, so I'd never consider Astrid a shag candidate. But the vampire she's dancing with is new here, her hair the color of spring lilacs.

Leaning over the balcony, I take in the baby vamp. She's dressed like a nun, but I admire how her unconstrained tits bounce in opposition to the rest of her body. Her nipples have turned hard, against the friction of her unflattering dress. She's not the best dancer, but there's something wild and free about how she moves to the music. I can't keep my eyes off her.

The DJs play modern tracks in this club most nights. The majority of vamps who come here prefer to live in the present, un-nostalgic for their pasts. Not me. I'd give my left nut to go back to the 1960s in London. Wild days those were... I should never have left.

I shake my head. I do miss that era, but if I could turn back time, I wouldn't change a thing. If I'd stayed in London I'd be an old man now. Fuck that.

"Like what you see?"

I turn to find Malcolm beside me, a knowing grin on his mug. My friend knows exactly where I was looking.

"Whatever do you mean?" I straighten off the balustrade.

He chuckles. "Listen. I need a favor."

"What kind of favor?"

"It involves the purple-haired baby vamp."

My eyes widen, making no attempt to hide my interest. "I'm listening."

"Her name's Selina. She lost her Maker before she was weaned. She needs to feed from a vamp, but from someone I trust."

"What makes you think you can trust me?"

My cock throbs at the mere thought of shagging that pretty young thing. There are dozens of hot birds in the club tonight, always are, and I have lots of options beyond Kara who's already offered, but it's clear what my free-ranging dick wants. It wants Selina.

CHAPTER
FIFTEEN

Selina

Astrid leads me off the dance floor and through the lounge behind it. Then we pass through a set of sheer curtains.

Behind the curtains, we're surrounded by sofas, in coverings as diverse as velvet and latex, and many are occupied by couples, couples and small groups of vampires engaged in... well, just about every sexual act I've ever imagined—and many I haven't.

I don't know where to look. To my right, a woman has a finger buried in the ass of a male whose penis is deep in the mouth of another male who's being penetrated from behind by yet another. Their movements are inconceivably fast, just like some of the sex I saw in Xavier's court, and yet somehow all four of them are working in tandem, like there's another soundtrack playing at ten times the speed of the club's thumping music.

To my right, a woman's sitting on the lap of a man, riding his erection with such speed I know the motion is faster than the human eye could detect—and all the while, their fangs are dug into each other's necks. How do they keep from ripping out each other's throats?

Astrid leans over and whispers. "You okay?"

I nod. "I didn't realize this was a... a *sex* club." My nerves are threatening to overtake my driving need for blood.

"It's not a sex club." She smiles. "Not really. Sometimes people get carried away when they feed."

"In public?"

Astrid chuckles. "This isn't exactly what I'd call *public.* And see all the doors?"

I shift my focus to the walls, only then noticing the lounge is lined by dozens of doors.

"Each leads to a private room."

"Oh." Fear overtakes my thirst. Am I going to be alone in one of those rooms with a vampire I've just met? What if he tries to rape me while I'm feeding? Worse, what if I don't want to stop him?

"There they are!" Astrid takes my hand and leads me across the room toward Malcolm, who's standing with an elegant vampire in a business suit.

The vampire is white, with neatly trimmed sideburns, but no beard or mustache. His hair, thick and dark, is parted on the right, long on the top but shorter on the sides, and dark waves drape casually across one of his strong eyebrows. His appearance is relaxed, but at the same time intentionally put together. His fine-boned facial features, his posture and his clothes all combine to make him very refined. Sophisticated and out of another time. As a vampire, he undoubtedly is.

The vampire smiles as we approach, and his gaze washes deliciously over my body, making me want to touch him, touch myself. I clasp my hands behind my back.

"Hello," he says in what sounds like a faint British accent. "You must be Selina." He holds his hand toward me and bows slightly.

I release one of my hands to take his, but instead of shaking it, like I expect, he increases his bow and gently kisses the back of my fingers.

At the touch of his lips, a shockwave of electricity tightens the place between my legs and it radiates outward. I gasp.

He straightens and turns to Malcolm. "She's utterly delightful."

I gather my wits. "Nice to meet you, um, I didn't catch your name."

"Grayson Cumberland the fourth at your service." He bows again.

I grin. I haven't yet worked out whether his formal demeanor is real or mocking. I suspect it's a little of both.

"Gray's an old friend," Malcolm tells me. "You'll be in good hands."

"The best." He holds them in front of me, then he wiggles his index and middle fingers together, just slightly. Heat shoots through me again.

What is going on with my body?

"I'm just here to feed," I say bluntly. "Nothing else."

"Yes," Astrid interjects. "Be good, Gray. A friend of ours is in love with Selina."

In love? Joy rushes through me. Did Rock tell her that? Is it true or is she just saying that to make her point?

"Don't worry, I will be, as ever, the consummate gentleman." His clothes say gentleman, but the look he shoots me doesn't. "And my vein is at your service, pet."

I frown, unsure I like his mocking tone or condescending nickname, but then he bends toward me, inhales deeply and whispers against my ear, “Don’t be afraid. I’ll take very good care of you. I promise.” His breath snakes over my neck and into my hair, and my back undulates as if his hands are caressing my body.

My breasts grow heavy and sensitive, and I cross my arms over my chest, hoping to hide my obvious arousal.

“Shall we find a room?” Grayson asks, and panic clenches inside me.

I look at Astrid, who steps forward. “No private room, okay? Selina would rather stay where Malc and I can see you two.”

“Your wish is my command.” He grins, then reaches toward me. “Shall we?”

His long, manicured fingers beckon me, and I stare for what is probably too long before taking his extended hand.

Grayson lightly guides me across the room to a velvet couch in a dark corner. “Is this location acceptable?”

I turn back to see Astrid and Malcolm seated across the room in a spot with a clear view of us. They seem dangerously far away, but at this moment so does Grayson’s vein. I want it under my fangs. Now.

He sits on the sofa, then pats the cushion next to him. “Come on, pet. I won’t bite.” I sit and he leans over, his lips near my ear. “Not unless you invite me to.”

A shiver races through me, but I turn toward him and smile. “That’s not likely. Sorry.”

He leans back, stretching one arm along the arm of the sofa, the other along its back behind me. “No apologies required.” His deep blue eyes flash with mischief, intelligence and utter sexiness. “You’re the one in charge. How do you want me?”

Hard and fast and right now. Where did that thought come from? The only man I want is Rock.

But there's something else I need from Grayson.

"I might..." I shake my head. "I'm not sure how this is done."

He blinks in obvious surprise but it quickly changes to a soft delight. His hand traces down the side of my cheek, and I lean into his caress, marveling at how good it feels.

"Just tell me where you want my vein." He tips his head to the side.

My chest rises and falls as I ponder what's about to happen and how I can best keep things from seeming sexual.

"I promise to keep my hands to myself," he says. "In fact, we can make sure of it." He removes his deep red necktie and hands it to me. Standing, he removes his suit jacket and lays it carefully over the arm of a nearby chair, then he undoes the top few buttons of his shirt, stopping when he gets halfway down.

I try not to pant, unsure of how his removing his clothes is going to help him keep his hands to himself, but not wanting to stop him.

"Do you mind if I remove this garment?" he asks. "It's Egyptian cotton, custom tailored. I'd rather not risk a bloodstain."

"That's fine." My voice comes out hoarse and quiet. I'm so thirsty I could drink a gallon—of anything—but what I most want is Grayson's blood, and as the moment draws near, my need grows even stronger. My fangs spring out, and a low growl rises from my throat.

"My goodness." He smiles. "Someone's getting impatient." He turns, putting his arms behind his back and lifting them toward me. "Tie me up. Make sure I keep my hands to myself."

Relief floods through me at his willingness to be tied up.

I'm frightened by my out-of-control libido that wants this sexy vampire's hands on me—and in me.

And I'm even more frightened by *his* desire. Desire that's clear in his eyes.

With him tied up I'll be the one in control. I can keep this all about feeding and ignore my misplaced lust. Hopefully the feeding will get rid of that longing, too.

As I bind his hands I fight the urge to lean into him, to rub my cheek on his strong body and feel the ridges of muscle that bunch when he pulls his hands back. He's slender, but strong, and I long to trace my tongue over all the ridges that form his back and arms and neck.

When I finish, he tests my knot, demonstrating that he can't pull his arms apart. Although I suspect he could if he really tried.

He turns toward me, a luscious smile on his lips, then returns to the sofa and sits, adjusting his arms behind him as he leans back. "This way okay? Or should I recline against the arm?" He nods to the side.

If he lies against the arm, I'll have to lie down on top of him to reach his neck. In his current position, I can kneel beside him on the sofa. Seems safer than straddling him. "That looks fine."

He nods, then exposes his vein.

Kneeling, I slide in close beside him. My heart is thumping out of control, and its beat mimics my overpowering urge to devour him in every way possible. A need that feels shameful and wrong, but at the same time so right.

Seeking support, I place my hand on his shoulder, and he sighs at the contact but doesn't move.

My position might be less awkward if I straddled him, but his woolen pants are already straining to contain an obvious erection. I don't want to lead him on or cause him any discomfort.

Leaving one hand on his shoulder, I cradle the back of his head. His hair is soft and longer on the sides than it first looked and slicked back with some kind of gel, I realize as I thread my fingers through the curls. Slowly, I move my mouth close to his throat.

His blood is pounding, coursing underneath the surface and calling out to me as strongly as Pike's did when I was starving.

I banish Pike from my thoughts and inhale, loving the smell, the spicy, fresh and incredibly male scent of Grayson. I lick his protruding vein.

Moaning, he adjusts his body, and his movement alarms me for a second, but he stays passive. Passive and yielding and utterly sexy.

I bite.

The instant my fangs dig into his skin I feel an ecstatic release. My entire body pulses with pleasure and a heightened hunger. Swallowing gulps so large they nearly choke me, I suck on the hot liquid that's pouring from his vein and into my mouth and down my throat. My mind floats on a river of pure pleasure and joy.

Then power surges through my body, a power I've never felt before, my muscles tripling in size, nerves finding new pathways, brain building new synapses.

And all those feelings are nothing compared to what's happening between my legs...

Gasping between gulps I realize the pressure against my sex isn't my imagination. It's his erection. In spite of my plans, I straddled Gray as I drank, and I'm rubbing his length with so much force I might crush him.

But instead of being crushed, he thrusts against me, meeting each of my undulations with equal force.

"Selina," he groans. "Baby. You'd better slow down or you'll suck me dry."

I stop feeding. Releasing my fangs from his throat, I lick his wounds as they heal. But although I had enough control to stop feeding, I'm utterly unable to keep my hips from sliding, from grinding and pressing his thickness hard against my sex.

I've never felt like this. So powerful, so alive, so turned on.

I want Grayson. Now. I want him to fuck me, to use me however he wants and for as long as he wants. I want to use him, too.

Use him for more than I already have used him, that is. And boy did I use him. Every cell in my body is sparking with the power I found in his blood, and my sex is deriving unbelievable pleasure against his erection.

"Did you get your fill?" His voice is soft in my ear. "Because if you need more, if you permit me to feed from you—just a taste—then I'll gain enough energy for you to take more."

I hike up the hem of my dress so that my panties are in better contact with his ridge, and I thrust against him, rubbing up and down his length, loving how the head of his penis strikes each time I reach the top. No matter how long I keep this up, I'll never get enough.

"Yes." I pant. "Yes. Feed from me. Take whatever you need."

In a flash, I'm on my back, his fangs against my neck and his pelvis grinding even more aggressively into my sex. Now he's on top, the angle's more direct and he strikes my clit with each hard stroke.

Pleasure grows inside. I'm going to come. I want to come.

He strokes his fangs along the side of my neck.

My orgasm explodes, sweeping me away as we grind our bodies together, but before I can ride out my climax, and before he can bite, it's all over.

Gray's body flies back from mine and topples over the other end of the sofa. Astrid stands over me, looking down with concern in her eyes.

"Shit, Gray." Malcolm unties Gray's hands as the latter kneels beyond the end of the sofa. "You said you wouldn't. You promised."

Gray looks into my eyes with so much intensity I feel like he's actually inside me, and I squirm, wishing Malcolm and Astrid would vanish, wishing I'd opted for that private room. And most of all, wishing I could free Gray's throbbing cock from his pants and thrust it inside me, right now.

I want that even more badly than I wanted his blood. But as we stare into each other's eyes, his expression softens, grows less hungry, and my breathing slows, too.

"It's okay," I tell Astrid and Malcolm, while still looking at Gray. "I told him he could feed. He kept his promise. It's not his fault."

Gray licks his lips, his eyes half closing as if just his tongue on my skin was the best thing he's ever tasted.

"Okay then," Astrid says. "*That* was exciting." She rolls her eyes looking at Gray. "Put that thing away, will you?"

Still on his knees, Gray adjusts himself. I hear a zipper and my insides cry as I rise to my knees, hoping for a better view, but I'm too late. I thought he'd been covered the whole time. Did *I* open his fly? His hands were tied. I must have.

I rise to my feet and sway, unused to the new power coursing inside me. Astrid steadies me.

"How about we go to the ladies' to freshen up." She puts her hand around my waist.

I follow her, more like stumble beside her, and the entire way I look over my shoulder, unable to take my eyes off Gray.

~

Selina

I LEAN AGAINST THE LADIES' room counter, trying to get my heart rate and breathing back to normal. My underwear is soaked and I try to resist squirming, my arousal is still off the charts.

"What's happening to me?" I ask her. "Why did I do that? I love Rock."

She rubs my shoulder. "I know, baby. But what just happened is perfectly normal."

I draw long, sucking breaths, trying to return my body to a state that I recognize. Then I freeze, realizing what I said. I used the L word about Rock, and as crazy as it seems after knowing him such a short time, I meant it.

It doesn't feel right that I told Astrid before telling Rock, but the idea of confessing my feelings to Rock sends another wave of anxiety coursing through me. I've already trusted him with my life. Can I trust him with my heart?

Everyone in my life who claimed to love me—my mother, the stepmonster, Xavier—they all hurt me in ways beyond belief. I don't trust love.

Something is broken inside me, and what I just did with Gray proves it.

"How is this *normal*?" I ask Astrid. "I don't even *know* Gray. I barely talked to him before we...before I..." I shake my head. "How did I get so out of control?"

She pulls me over to a chaise at the side of the room and we sit, her holding my hands. "Lots of people have strong reactions the first time they drink from a vampire who's not their Maker, and..." She glances away.

"And what?" I prod. "I need to learn."

She nods, looking me directly in the eyes. "Passion during feeding is common. It can build strong bonds."

"So, now I've got some kind of *bond* with this guy?" I say the words with horror, but in truth it doesn't sound so bad. I must still be under the effects of his blood.

She shakes her head. "What you're feeling right now is lust. It will wear off." She bites her lower lip. "But..."

"But what?"

"I've never seen Gray like that before. That's why we chose him for you. Over the decades, I've seen him with plenty of women and a few men, too. He's popular. He can get anyone he wants, but I've never seen him so...so utterly absorbed."

I try to hide how happy her words make me. I wish I could hide it from myself.

"What?" Astrid says. "You seem conflicted. What are you thinking? Tell me."

"What I said about Rock before. That I love him." I shake my head. "I can't explain how that happened so quickly. I haven't even told Rock, so you can't say anything, please. Not even to Malcolm."

She nods, making a lock-turning motion in front of her half-smiling lips.

"But I do love Rock, and I can't imagine my life without him." I look down at my hand, interlaced with hers.

"What?" She tucks a finger under my chin and raises my gaze to meet hers. "What's wrong?"

"If you and Malcolm hadn't stopped us, I would have had *sex* with Gray. I get the whole attraction while-you're-feeding thing... And you're right, that's wearing off a bit."

"And yet you still feel something for Gray," she says without accusation, without any kind of judgment.

I nod. "It seems...so wrong. Like I'm betraying Rock."

"Honey. Lots of vampires take multiple mates. You know that."

"Females, too?" Xavier had eighteen mates, but I never imagined it the other way around.

"Of course," she answers.

"You and Malcolm?"

"Neither of us has met anyone else we want to mate. We give each other everything we need."

"That's what I want." I squeeze her hand. "I want what you and Malcolm have. A monogamous committed relationship with a man that I love."

"The heart wants what the heart wants." She cups my face. "Don't fight your feelings."

"What do you mean by that?"

"I mean you should stop worrying. Listen to your heart, not a bunch of rules you learned when you were human. If you listen to your heart, I promise you'll find your mate—or mates. You'll find the ones who will make you happy."

CHAPTER SIXTEEN

Gray

Malcolm ushers me toward the side of the room as the ladies head in the other direction. Selina stares back at me with longing in her eyes that makes me want to follow, to drag her away from Astrid and fuck her over and over, never stopping until we die.

"What the fuck, man?" Malcolm says.

"Don't look at me." I shake my head. "I didn't start it." But that's no excuse. She's a baby. I should have been able to prevent that from happening. I should have shown more control.

"It was her first time!" Malcolm says. "You knew that."

"I know." I rake back my hair, still trying to get in control of my body, my emotions. "My hands were tied."

"That's some bullshit excuse and you know it."

I do know it. I could have broken the bonds holding my hands in an instant. I could have put a stop to her dry humping, but if I'm being honest with myself, if I'd broken free the situation would have quickly moved past dry humping. Way past.

I scared Selina. I nearly *shagged* her. Given another two seconds, my fangs would have been in her vein, those panties would have been off her and then...

No wonder that Xavier creep wanted her. Selina's intoxicating. Beautiful, yes, but her inherent power... There's something different about her.

I shake my head. As she pulled blood from my vein it was nearly impossible to believe she hadn't gained power from the veins of a thousand vampires before me, and while she fed, I felt a strength in her that compared only to Faiza, the one who made me.

No vampire I've met since has lived up to even an ounce of Faiza's power or sensuality. And none has ever touched my heart. I thought my Maker had spoiled me for love. Until tonight.

I stare at the ladies' room door. "What do you think Astrid's saying to her?"

"I don't know, you asshole. Probably trying to convince her that you aren't a rapist."

"Hey, I was the one with my hands tied. If anyone was a potential rapist in that situation..."

Malcolm shoots me a look, and I hold up my hands in surrender. "Okay. Okay. But man...you're sure it was her first time feeding from a vampire?" Her reaction was way stronger than I expected, and I nearly took advantage of her inexperience.

"She claims she didn't even feed from her Maker."

"That's not possible."

"I know," Malcolm says. "But her transition story is compelling. I was going to suggest she tell you about it, too, in case you have any theories, but after what just went down, I'm not sure you should ever get within a mile of her again."

He's right, but I don't want to stay away from her, either. I close my eyes for a moment as a theory of how she might have turned takes hold in my mind. It doesn't seem possible, and my suspicion fills me with dread.

But if she's telling the truth, there's only one explanation that makes any sense. I had a strange feeling from the moment I met her, one that should have thrilled me given my mission, but I don't like it. I don't like it one bit.

Malcolm claps my shoulder. "Can you keep your dick in your pants from now on?"

I nod.

"Because Selina needs our help, Gray. That Xavier asshole sent his so-called King's Guard after her. She needs to learn how to defend herself and you're the most highly skilled fighter I know. Rock can't protect her on his own."

Power surges inside me, along with the need to keep Selina safe—at any cost. My instinct to protect her is so strong I don't mind if Malcolm's friend is protecting her, too. And if my suspicions are right, my need to protect her goes way beyond my attraction. Keeping her safe is my duty.

"I'll help train her," I tell Malcolm. "You were right to come to me, mate. What happened tonight..." I hold up my hands. "It won't happen again."

But now that I've inhaled Selina's scent, felt her soft body against mine, I *have* to see her again, even if I'm forced to remain chaste. I can keep my distance. I have to.

"I'll keep my hands off her like it's my sworn duty."

Malcolm snorts.

Selina exits the ladies' room behind Astrid, and my cock instantly springs to attention, so hard it's painful. I twist my back against the wall, hoping to find a position where my raging wood isn't touching my trousers, some posture where my arousal isn't so fucking obvious.

If I'm going to help train Selina, I'll have to find a way to live with constant wood.

And I'll be able to confirm my theory. If I'm right, I'll be lauded, rewarded beyond my wildest dreams, but the thought of completing my mission fills me with loss.

If I'm right, I can never be with her. Not ever.

CHAPTER SEVENTEEN

Selina

My heart jumps when I see Rock step out from the tree's shadow, but as he crosses the street, guilt floods through me. I run to him and fall into his arms, pressing my head against his thick chest.

"What's wrong?" he asks. Lifting me, he takes a strong step toward his vampire friends. "What did you do to her?"

"She's fine," Astrid says. "She fed from someone we know and trust and—"

"I'll tell him about it." I lift my head from Rock's chest. "The feeding was intense, but I'm absolutely fine. I'm just so glad to see you."

Holding me aloft in front of him, he searches my eyes for answers, and I hope he finds the reassurance he needs there, because in his eyes I see the lengths he would go to protect me.

I will tell him what happened with Gray, but first I need to tell him how I feel about him. As soon as we get home.

Even if he doesn't reciprocate my feelings, knowing that he feels protective will be enough for me. I'll make it be enough.

He sets me down, then wraps an arm around my shoulders, the weight and heat welcome burdens.

"Your British friend," Rock says to the other vampires. "What's his name again? Grayson? He's on his way over."

My insides go berserk watching Gray walk down the path from the house toward us. Out here in the moonlight, he's even more handsome, unnaturally so, and he strides with a combination of confidence and grace that anyone would find alluring.

Gray slowly opens the gate to the sidewalk and joins the four of us at the edge of the street.

"Rock, right?" Gray reaches out his hand, and my giant takes it, the two males shaking like it's an Olympic event and both want the gold.

"Gray's agreed to help with Selina's training," Malcolm says.

"Do I get a say in that?" I ask.

Gray's face flashes with what looks like hurt, but it's gone so quickly I wonder whether or not it was my imagination.

"Gray was made by one of the Ancients," Malcolm tells me. "And he's trained in every martial art invented by human or vampire. Plus, his knowledge of vampiric history could answer some questions about how you were turned."

"Not to mention," Astrid adds, "why that Xavier guy was so determined to have you as his mate."

I nod. Until now, it never occurred to me that anything was driving Xavier beyond malice, his anger at my refusal to yield. Could there be more? If so, I'm in even more danger than I imagined.

"We need somewhere to train," Gray says.

"The gym at FJS." Malcolm looks at Gray like it's obvious.

"No." Gray shakes his head. "Too many people could spot her there."

"So what?" Astrid widens her stance. "Xavier's Guard hasn't infiltrated FJS. She'll be safe at FJS."

"Still..." Gray says. "Somewhere less conspicuous would be better. I know a warehouse—"

"I've got a place," Rock interrupts. "Below my bar."

"A basement gym?" Gray's tone is beyond condescending. "Forgive me giant, but you have no idea what it takes to train a vampire princess."

Everyone turns toward him, including me.

"*Princess*?" Astrid says. "Are you serious, Gray? You said you'd be nice."

Gray laughs, but it's an awkward laugh, and instead of taking back yet another condescending nickname for me, he doubles down. "What else should I call such an inexperienced baby who needs all four of us to help her?"

Crushed by his patronizing expression and tone, I double down, too. I step away from Rock, back straight, head high, all my muscles taut so no one can see them tremble.

"For all you know, Grayson Cumberland the fourth, I *am* a princess." I point toward him. "Watch yourself or I'll make you kneel before me."

He sucks in a sharp breath, then turns on the charm. "Okay, princess. You win." Grinning, he kneels and shuffles toward me. If his smile weren't so charming, this playacting would make me even angrier. But instead, I want him to shuffle that smiling face right between my legs.

Cheeks blazing, legs quivering, I turn away from the vampire kneeling before me. "I feel safe at Rock's."

"Your wish is my command. *Princess*." Gray says the last word mockingly.

"When do we start?"

Rock smiles. "I say today. How's nine?"

"As in *morning*?" Gray gets up from his knees and shakes his head as he brushes dirt off his expensive-looking suit. "What time is it now?"

"Four-twenty," Malcolm replies.

"I need to go home and change into something a little more...appropriate." Gray frowns. "Doesn't give me much time to get there before dawn."

Rock grunts. "I thought vampires were fast."

"We are at some things," Gray says. "Other things?" He shoots me a wicked smile. "With certain things, we vampires like to take our time, making them *last* like no other species on Earth can."

"Gray," Astrid says. "You're terrible."

He backs away, hands up again. "Can't help myself, luv."

The meaning of his words sinks in, and I feel like a child for not figuring it out sooner. Gray was bragging about sex. How long he can last. Flames lick inside me, thinking about him taking his time—with me—taking his time as he thrusts deep inside me.

Burning up, I back toward Rock, and he slings his arm around my waist, pulling me tightly against him.

They call me a baby, and I *am* a child compared to all four of them. I don't know any of their actual ages, but can sense that they were made many years ago. And if Gray was made by one of the Ancients...

I don't know what that means, not precisely, but the

idea isn't hard to comprehend. I assume Gray's at least as old as Rock, maybe older, even though he looks like he's in his twenties.

It's a strange new world I live in, one where appearances count for nothing—not when it comes to guessing ages, anyway.

"Show up or don't," Rock says. "I can teach her to fight."

"She needs to know more than how to throw a punch, big man. It's not like she can sit on her opponents, which I would imagine is your preferred fighting tactic."

Rock's hold tightens on my ribs. "If you think you know better, then show up." His fingers ripple over my ribs, barely moving, but each adjustment ignites little sparks of pleasure inside me. I can't wait to get back to Rock's.

My libido has revved up again and, if I'm honest, it never really calmed down after what happened on that sofa. Plus, I sense that the feeding altered something deep inside me. My sex drive is even stronger, and everything else about me feels stronger too, like it will never go back to normal.

"Thanks for the meal," I say to Gray as coldly as I can manage.

But as much as I try to stay neutral, Gray's expression is so hungry when he looks back at me that I need to turn away.

"Thank you, Malcolm and Astrid," I say. "It was lovely meeting you and I really appreciate all your help."

"You're welcome," Astrid says as she takes her mate's hand. "Now we'd all better get out of this street before someone notices us and calls the cops."

"Or we fry in the sun," Malcolm adds.

"Wait!" Gray's posture changes, his muscles tense and

his nose lifts to bring in more of the night air as he scans the street. "Someone's here. Someone's watching us."

"The police?" Astrid asks, looking around herself. "Xavier's Guard?"

Fear seizes my chest and Rock holds me more tightly.

"Never mind," Gray says. "Whoever it was, they're gone." He delivers the words with assurance, but his body language, still tense, hints at something different.

"In any case—" he nods to Rock "—best get her home quickly."

Selina

After the potent cocktail of adrenaline and sex hormones, not to mention the dash back to Rock's bar, filled with fear that Pike found me, I'm full of energy when we return.

I need to talk to Rock. I need to tell him how much I care about him. And to explain what happened with Grayson, or try to, before I have to resist that irresistible vampire while we're training. Rock will probably pick up on our sexual tension, and besides that, he deserves to know.

Even if the chemistry between Grayson and me is dialed down by a hundred when we train tomorrow, I need Rock to understand that what I feel for Gray isn't real. That it's just a vampire thing. That the one I truly want is him.

Stretching, Rock yawns. "If we're going to train in the morning, we'd better get a few hours of sleep. I'll take the couch."

"No." I step slowly toward him. "You don't need to give up your bed." I lean against him.

He keeps his arms at his sides, but I cradle into the vast

expanse of his chest feeling like I fit there. Like the space between his huge pecs was custom made for my head.

I can think of other ways I hope we'll fit, too, but I want to take things slowly. Not only for me, but I sense for him, too. This thing with Rock, whatever it is, it's too important to rush. It has the potential to not only be my first relationship, but the one that lasts for the rest of my life.

"Can we talk for a bit before bed?"

Rock sits on the sofa, and I snuggle in beside him.

"Hey," I ask softly. "Do you think that Grayson guy will show up for training?" I try to keep my mention of Gray casual, like I couldn't care less.

"Got the feeling he's pretty motivated to come."

"But how...how will he get in?" It's getting close to dawn and the bar is locked.

"He can find out."

I turn toward him. "Gray's been here before?"

"In the bar, yes. Not sure if he's been in the gym, but a lot of vamps know about my gym and how to get in. Everyone who works at FJS knows or can easily find out."

"Really? Why?"

"O'Malley's is a vamp sanctuary. Available for anyone who needs to escape the sun or the cops."

"Wow." That's really generous and kind of Rock. He keeps exceeding all of my expectations. By multiples. "Isn't that a big risk for you? Sheltering vampires? If the cops find out..."

He shrugs. "I trust my staff, and I trust the vamps who come here."

I fondle the front of Rock's shirt, lightly skirting over the surface and loving how his heart rates increase under my ear, at my light touch.

That he risks his bar, his life, to help vampires he

doesn't even know... My feelings for Rock are so strong, and I have to find a way to tell him. Even if it seems way too soon.

I freeze and straighten.

"What's wrong?" he asks, concern in his eyes.

"If your sanctuary is well known amongst the vampire community, then...could Pike find it? Could he find me down here?"

Rock's huge fingers stroke my back as he ponders my question, or how best to answer it.

"I've thought of that," he says softly.

"You have?"

He nods. "But don't worry."

"How can I not worry?" Rock is strong, but Pike... A shudder traces through me. Pike might not be as large as my giant, but he's ferocious and a vampire. And if he comes in while we're sleeping...

"First off," Rocks says, "the gym that's one floor above us is well known, but no one knows how to get down to this level. No one has the code or even knows where the door is. You're the only person I've ever brought down here. Ever."

My heart flutters. "Not even Malcolm or Astrid?"

He shakes his head.

"Or Chelle?"

"Chelle?" His head snaps back. "Why would she ever come down here?"

"Just wondering." Knowing I'm the only one who's been down here warms me inside, gives me hope that Rock might feel as strongly about me as I do about him.

"And the second?"

"Second?" he asks.

"You said first off."

"Oh, yeah. Right. Well, I admit I was worried last night.

Barely slept. I had this strange feeling that someone was watching. Watching the whole time, even when I first threw that guy off you in the alley."

"You did?" I snuggle in more closely, fear creeping in.

"Yeah. But..."

"But what?"

"I think that if I'm right and someone was watching, if it was that Pike guy, he'd have burst in here already, or tried to nab you upstairs in the bar or when we went out to the club."

"I guess that makes sense." And it does. If someone was watching us in the street tonight, or the alley last night, there's no way it was Pike. If it were Pike I'd already be dead —or much worse.

I relax into Rock's arms, trying to refocus on what I want to discuss. "Rock..."

"Yes?" He strokes my back.

"There's something I need to tell you."

"Something about what happened with that Grayson guy?" he asks softly.

I sit up to face him. "How do you know?"

"I don't. Not really." He shakes his head. "And it's none of my business."

"You don't care?"

"Why?" Rock's body straightens and his expression turns fierce. "Did he hurt you? Did he do anything uninvited?"

Uninvited? No direct invitation was ever issued, but I never said no. In fact, when I replay the events in my head, it was me who should have been asking for consent. I was the instigator. That's why I feel so guilty.

I shake my head. "No, he didn't do anything uninvited."

"Then it's all good." Rock smiles and strokes my hair. "If you're happy, I'm happy."

"But..."

"Acushla. I have no claim on you. Certainly no *exclusive* claim."

"But what if I *want* you to?" Feeling bold, I straddle Rock's broad lap. My legs aren't able to touch the sofa cushions on either side of his body, leaving my weight on my inner thighs as they spread over his expanse.

His muscles are tense and hard, especially on the left side where a ridge of muscle digs into my inner thigh. It's hard to even imagine the extent of the strength and power restrained inside Rock's body.

Desire fills his eyes, but he stays still, not even touching me anymore. "Selina, I..."

Fearing an objection, I interrupt his words with a kiss.

He doesn't respond, but I refuse to give up. Taking his head between my hands, I press my lips against his, kissing him hard and then soft, over and over, relishing his salty flavor. Rock tastes how I imagine the ocean tastes, or a mountain.

I am falling in love with this man, and I want to make love with him, too. I need to release tonight's built-up sexual tension and take our relationship to the next level. If I can't gather the courage to use words to tell Rock how I feel, I can show him through my actions, use my body to demonstrate all the emotions surging inside me.

And more than just emotions are rushing through me. My physical lust expands, building from an already hot need into something far stronger, something animalistic, something I fear I can't control.

Nibbling on Rock's lush lips, I bite lightly, and then

trace his mouth's seam with the tip of my tongue, urging it to open.

When it does, my tongue dives inside, and a rumble builds inside him, starting low where my belly is pressed against his and gaining in strength and volume, rising until it erupts in a groan against my mouth.

His hands fly to my head and he deepens our kiss, our lips devouring each other's, like neither of us will ever be satisfied.

My body rubs against his, the friction delicious yet not nearly enough, but from my position, the best I can do is grind against the button at the waistband of his jeans and although it's working for me, I need more. Plus I need him to feel good, too.

I fumble behind us, reaching down for his erection. He must be hard. But where is it? I stretch as my hand traces over the front of his jeans. I can't find my target, then I feel a twitch beneath my left thigh.

I gasp. The massive ridge of muscle I'm sitting on isn't thigh muscle. It's not part of his leg, it's *over* his leg. No wonder I feel lopsided.

I shift to the right and reach down to the area I exposed. As my fingers slide along the ridge, he hisses against my mouth. My cupped hand can't even span his massive erection as it rests against his leg, and I slowly slide my fingers toward the head, shocked that I haven't yet found it. In fact, I may not be able to reach far enough without breaking our kiss.

Desire pools between my legs even as fear builds in my head.

When I was captive at court, I was penetrated—forcefully—by large things, horrible things, but this... Rock is so big.

My fingers finally reach the tip, and I squeeze slightly. He groans and lifts me up, holding me dangling in front of him so I can no longer kiss him or reach where I want.

His eyes are filled with a heart-wrenching combination of desire and pain. I want to tell him that I love him. That I love him so hard, love him with an emotion so strong I can barely contain it.

"Rock..."

"Take off your panties."

I exhale roughly, my suspended body contracting involuntarily as his words penetrate me with pulsing pleasure. Pleasure followed by fear. I tamp down the fear. Even if the penetration's painful, even if he tears me, I'll heal, and I'll do anything to give this man pleasure. To show him I love him. *Anything*.

I tug down my panties and free one leg, but before I can liberate the other, his massive arms lift me higher, above his head.

Adjusting his hold on me, he moves one of his hands under my right leg. Then, leaning his torso forward on the sofa, he drapes my leg over his shoulder.

"What?" Holding my back, he scoops my other leg up over him too, and then pushes aside my dress until it's bunched above my waist.

His breath hot on my sex, I rest my hands on top of his head.

I've never had oral sex, but I've seen it done, though this position isn't something I've ever imagined.

"Acushla." He says the word so close to my body that I feel the displacement of air, and even that light touch sends a ripple of pleasure racing through me. "I want to taste you."

"Taste?" I gasp.

His tongue laps along one inner thigh, then the other, and my insides pulse. I'm so wet, I feel sure that I'm flowing like a tap right in front of him. He presses his lips against my mound and kisses me strongly, pulling even more blood to the area. I can barely think, barely breathe.

His tongue juts out and licks my pubic hair, teasing me, driving me wild, and then it plunges between my folds, landing on my clit and circling there.

I buck and cry out. The feeling's so fantastic. So much better than my finger or that ridge on the dungeon bench.

But before I come, he moves away from my clit, and his tongue trails through my folds, licking down one side and up the other, over and over.

My climax is so close, but his tongue shifts its attention from the edges of my folds to slide right down the center of me. It skims at first, then strokes more firmly, lingering every few passes to circle my opening and tease the sensitive nerves there.

After all the horrible sex in my life, all the repulsive things that have been done to hurt me, to control me or punish me...this, this one moment... If it never goes any further than this—this makes up for it all.

The speed of Rock's stroking accelerates, each pass grazing over both my opening and my clit, his tongue traveling back and forth between the two nerve-filled areas, but just as I'm about to explode, he slows down and starts kissing my labia instead, avoiding my most sensitive places. My hips move, encouraging his tongue, hungry for more.

When he finally licks my clit again, I gasp at the pleasure. His lips lock around the small bud, creating suction.

I never.... Oh. Wow.

My heels press against his back, and I want simultaneously to draw away from the intensity and get closer. Stars explode behind my eyes, and a thousand hot suns burst, burning me up from inside.

Rock adjusts his grip as my body convulses, as I writhe and grind and buck against his face, riding out an orgasm so intense that nothing I've ever felt or even imagined compares.

When my body finally starts to slow, he relaxes his grip. I'm panting, my insides still throbbing, wanting to feel that huge cock moving inside me. It's a good thing he got me well prepared.

His hand tightens around my waist and I get ready for him to lift me down, but instead he lifts me higher, and slides himself lower, so that his head's resting on the back of the sofa with my lower legs trapped between his shoulders and the cushion.

He adjusts me slightly, and then traces my opening again, making his tongue into a hard point as he strokes. The tightly rolled muscles generate different sensations than the flatter version, and I'm just getting used to it when his curled-up tongue pierces my opening.

Shocked by the unexpected penetration, I tense around it. He groans and the sound rumbles through his mouth to vibrate inside me.

Pulling down on my hips, he forces his tongue deeper, and I relax my inner muscles as he presses in and out of me, using his hands at my hips to gain traction, fucking me with his taut organ in a way that feels a million times better than any other kind of penetration I've ever experienced. It's not even in the same category of acts.

His tongue thrusts, over and over, and his hands hold me firmly above him as he continues to dive. My legs and hips get in on the action, until I'm bouncing on top of his face, like we've invented some wild kind of rodeo event.

Another orgasm builds deep inside me, tightening every muscle in my body at once and creating an ache deep inside me, like my womb is convulsing. All my muscles contract at once as the climax explodes, and I rest my forehead against the wall as my body contracts, greedily wanting every second of pleasure to be gleaned from his mouth.

After the last trace of orgasm shudders through me, I can't move. I know I should get off his face before I risk smothering him, but his tongue's still inside me, and each time he exhales my body tingles. I'm at the edge of wanting even more.

His tongue starts sliding again, slowly pulling all the way out, and then tracing my folds before piercing me quickly again. And after countless rounds of that, he pulls it out, lingering at the entrance and lightly licking me there.

"Oh, Rock," I sigh.

He pushes hard into me again.

His tongue curls and licks my inner wall, rubbing the tip firmly against the front of my vagina. Within seconds, I come again. As he rubs me inside, I pound on the wall behind him, and my entire body vibrates. Sparks fly from every nerve, shooting so far I expect the room to catch fire.

When my inner contractions finally subside, I shake with the aftershocks as he gently lowers me onto my back on the sofa. I spread my legs wide for him. As wide as the back of the sofa allows.

"I'm ready, Rock." I look into his desire-filled eyes. "I want to feel you inside me. I want to make you feel as good as you made me feel."

He shakes his head.

"Rock." I lift my head from the sofa. Is it time? Time to tell him I love him? That I'll do anything to make him happy?

He stands, pulls my dress down over my sex and rests his hand there, hot and heavy and comforting after so much stimulation.

"Acushla." He shakes his head. "I am not the man for you. I can never give you what you want. What you need. What you deserve. You deserve someone to fully love you and that man, it can never be me."

He backs away, and I curl up into myself, turning onto my side, wanting to drown in my sadness.

CHAPTER EIGHTEEN

Rock

Watching Selina sleep, my heart breaks in two. I brought her to sexual climax more than once tonight, but my tongue and even my fingers will never be enough. We can never complete the act of love that she craves, that she deserves.

But that repulsive act...

Nightmarish memories flood my mind and weaken my limbs. I stagger into my room and collapse against the dresser. My legs crumple under me, dropping me to a crouch, my hands cradling my head against my knees as the nightmare takes hold.

"Behold!" the barker announces like he does every night. "Behold the giant and his prodigious piston! Behold the beast let loose!"

The crowd cheers.

"And gentlemen, be warned," the barker continues. "Leave

your women behind. This show will cause all decent ladyfolk to collapse into a trance from which they will never awaken."

Every night, every show, no matter how many years passed, I trembled hearing these words. I still tremble now, at the memory. When the owner first conceived of my loathsome show, I was defiant, swearing I would never perform.

But soon they figured out a way to force me. Every night they'd torture my Lily until I complied. They'd threaten her and force me to hurt other women to protect the one I loved.

I squeeze my head, trying to crush the memories flooding back.

The curtain draws open, and the crowd cheers. Not for me. I'm still in the wings. The audience cheers for the poor, unsuspecting prostitute my handler hired.

My victim prances across the stage as instructed, her breasts bouncing above her bodice, her nipples garishly rouged and her skirts hiked up to reveal her split pantaloons.

She turns to expose her sex to the gathered men, spreading her legs as they cheer at her wiggling ass and glistening sex.

My handler, in the wings near me, growls, "Okay, monster. Time to get it up."

Bound by thick chains, I lunge at him, but he remains out of range.

"Oh! Look who's come to watch," the handler says, pointing into the wings on the other side of the stage.

I try not to look where he's pointing, but not looking won't stop them from touching her, hurting her.

Facing me from the other side of the stage is Lily. My love is encaged, naked, spread-eagled, her hands and feet bound, her mouth gagged.

"The whore is ready for you," the handler behind me says.

"Both whores, I should say." One of the men on the other side of the stage fondles Lily's body and she writhes, stretching against her bindings trying to escape his touch.

Coming up behind her, he makes rude thrusts as he pinches her nipples.

I choke down my reaction, knowing from experience that any show of anger will only turn his mock thrusts into real ones.

"Perform well," my handler says, "or the slut in the cage dies. But not until after the men have some fun while you watch." I know this line well. He says it to me every night. And I know he means it. The few nights I refused to perform, they made me watch while they raped her.

I cannot let that happen. Never again. Even if it means killing the woman on stage.

"Behold!" the barker cries out to the crowd.

He gives the prostitute a signal, and she bends over, parting the gap in her pantaloons to expose her sex to the men again.

They all cheer.

"As you can see," the barker says, "this woman has a normal-sized cunny." The crowd cheers and shouts lewd suggestions.

"May I have a volunteer to verify?" the barker calls out.

As always, nearly every man fights to get onstage.

The one chosen is asked to penetrate the woman's body with his finger and the woman squeals in staged delight.

"Is this gentleman's finger big?" the barker asks the prostitute.

She nods and feigns sexual ecstasy as the volunteer pumps his finger inside her. The crowd cheers.

"Could you take something bigger?" the barker asks and she vigorously shakes her head no.

"Oh, but I think she can. What do you say?" he asks the crowd, while holding up two fingers, then three.

Encouraged by the crowd, the man on stage adds more digits to his finger rutting. Sweat rises on the man's pudgy face and an obvious bulge rises in his pants.

"Thank you," the barker says to the volunteer. "I think that she's ready."

As the man's escorted off, an apparatus is rolled forward from the back of the stage. The woman's hands are manacled to it, then her feet, her body bent forward over a padded rail.

Why they bother padding the rail is beyond me. I suppose so that they can be seen as kind while I am the brute.

While all this is happening, I furiously rub my cock, wanting it not only hard, but ready to release. I know the consequences of walking on stage flaccid. Lily pays. And I want this to be over as quickly as possible.

"But," the barker says, "even if this lady's ready for a good rutting, can any cunt be truly ready for this?"

On cue, I walk on stage, my ankle chains clanging on the floor behind me, and one hand supporting my monstrous rod. The crowd gasps. They always gasp.

I fight the shame and rage coursing inside me, and I silently ask the woman for forgiveness, resolving to get the show over as quickly as possible. Anything I can do to shorten Lily's torture, not to mention my fellow performer's.

My only consolation—and it's small—is that my costume covers my face and some of my shame. But it covers little else. A leather mask shields my features, barely allowing me to see or breathe, and a few scant leather straps wrap around my body, all of them joined to the heavy chains I drag behind me. My constraints allow me to reach the woman, but go no farther.

The crank locks into place with a loud clang, as my handler stops me several feet away from her. I continue to rub myself, determined to climax fast, but not so fast I don't get inside her first. Lily will pay the price for that mistake, too.

"Has anyone ever seen such a steed?" the barker shouts. "Have any of you ever seen such a thick, long tool, even on an actual steed?"

A few in the crowd laugh, but mostly they've grown silent, drawing closer to the stage. Some of them quite obviously thrust their hands into their pants.

The barker spins the apparatus holding the woman so she can see me and my fully engorged member. Her eyes fill with terror and she struggles, trying to release her bonds. I have no idea what they tell the women they hire for my show, or how they continue to find any willing in any town we visit.

Some nights the woman assumes the show is a joke, or some kind of a magic trick, and plays along, pretending to be excited, right up until the moment I ram into her.

But tonight the woman's terrified. After she gets a look at my shame, she struggles hard against her constraints.

The barker turns the apparatus around, so her ass is toward me again, and I hear the crank of the wheel as it releases my chains to give my range another few feet.

The barker continues to rile up the crowd, although at this point, they need little encouragement. Nor do I, as I watch one of the monsters in Lily's cage flick a bullwhip close beside her, as another man traces an electrified rod, meant for cattle, up her legs, threatening to impale her.

I will not let that happen.

I press two of my fingers inside the woman, two fingers that together have more girth than most men's rigid cocks. The woman cries out and squeezes against me.

Gagged, I can't tell her how sorry I am, so instead, I vigorously rub her insides, making her as aroused as possible, and then I use the lubrication from inside her to better prepare my cock. Not that any amount of lubrication could ever prepare a woman's cunny for a giant's cock.

The man shocks one of Lily's inner thighs. I can't stall any longer.

Holding the wooden apparatus for leverage, I use my other hand to hover my huge member against her entrance.

Then I thrust. I thrust and thrust, knowing the action is tearing her, knowing her blood is providing extra lubrication.

Wanting it to be over as fast as it can be, I close my eyes and grab the apparatus with both hands so I can pump hard and fast to completion. Only when I withdraw a flaccid cock will they release my Lily.

My mind returns to the present and my chest heaves with sobs. I pound my back against the dresser, relishing the pain from the knobs as they dig into my spine. It's nothing compared to the pain I've caused so many.

And I did that show nightly. Nightly for *years and years,* until one night they accidentally killed my love.

And just as it did then, the mere idea of sex makes my stomach turn. My cock remained flaccid for decades. Until her. Until Selina.

But I can never—ever—do to Selina what I did to those women. I can never make love to her like a proper man should.

And I am falling in love with her, so hard and so quickly.

In time I feel sure I will love Selina as much as I loved my Lily. But Selina and I can never perform the act of love. And that act is a fundamental need for her species. Vampires need sex as strongly as they need blood.

I will never be able to offer her what she needs. The best I can do is protect her from all those who would harm her —especially myself.

CHAPTER NINETEEN

Selina

The night air is humid and cool as it fills my lungs.

I beckon to someone. Behind me, a young woman smiles at me as she follows. "Where are we going?" she asks.

I don't answer, but she follows me anyway as I trail my hand along the back of a park bench, then round it to sit. Across from the park is a massive tree, behind that tall hedge enclosing the yard of a large brick house. The street and park are deserted. It's very late.

As soon as the young woman sits beside me, I lean forward, grab her head and bite.

I wake on Rock's couch, my body thrashing.

Regaining consciousness, I sit up and put my hands on my head. My mouth is so dry I can barely get the roof of my mouth to release my tongue. That dream was so vivid, like no other dream I've ever had.

Are nightmares another side effect of feeding from a vampire? I shake my head. If vivid dreaming is a side effect of anything, it's more likely my sexual frustration. I stare toward Rock's bedroom, but he made it clear he doesn't love me and won't give me what I want. Maybe ever.

Selina

Our sixth day in the gym, Rock charges at me full speed.

Just as he's within arm's reach, I tuck and roll, planning to trip him, but he anticipates my move and easily jumps over my tumbling body. He turns, then scoops me up as I stand, and he pins my back against his body, my arms against my sides.

"Good try on the evasive tactics, princess," Gray calls out from where he's leaning against the wall. "But we need to work on your *offense*."

Unable to move my arms, I roll my head back toward Rock, who still holds me. I breathe in his musky, sweaty scent, trying to touch him in any way I can with the few parts of me I can move.

He drops me to the mat.

From the side of the room, Gray chuckles, and I give him the finger.

The three of us have trained together for the past six days, at least five hours each day, but neither man will touch me. Not in the way that I want them to.

Rock's been teaching me to wrestle and street fight, while Gray's showing me how to use my speed and agility, and how to make the most of martial arts. While the combat training puts us in close quarters, it only leaves me wanting more. More from *both* of them. Which is crazy. Crazy for multiple reasons.

After using his tongue to give my body the most intense pleasure imaginable, Rock broke my heart. He said he could never love me, and now he's acting as if it never happened and refusing to even talk about what happened that night. And even worse, he's refused to touch me again, even though we're essentially living together with me crashing on his couch.

After that first night, Rock insisted I take the bed, but I crept out of the bedroom to join him on the sofa, so he gave up, took the bedroom and locked the door. Luckily vampires don't need to pee, or I'd have to go up a few flights of stairs and use the ladies' room in the bar.

And Gray... As much as I know I love Rock—I've never been more certain of anything in my life—I can't fight my desire for Gray.

The vampire saunters toward me now and reaches down to help me to my feet. As I rise, I purposefully let myself go off balance and fall against him.

As he catches me, his teeth scrape the side of my neck, and he inhales audibly. He might try to hide it, but clearly the physical attraction is mutual. I arch into him, my body wanting Gray, even if my mind tells me there's no use.

He lifts me away from him. "Nice try, princess."

"Stop calling me that."

He smirks.

Such a patronizing nickname from a man would normally enrage me, but with Gray it's like motivation. It makes me want to prove that I'm *not* a princess, that I'm tough, that I'm not the baby he thinks I am. I'm a fully grown woman who knows what she wants. What she *needs*.

Desire stirs inside me.

Rock's cellphone buzzes and he grabs it from a wooden bench.

He frowns. "Gotta go upstairs to take a delivery. Keep working." He strides toward the exit that leads out of the gym, hidden at the back of his bar's storage area.

Neither Malcolm nor Astrid came today and for the first time, I'm alone with Gray.

I slowly turn toward the vampire. Can I seduce him? Do I dare?

He comes at me with a twisting kick, his whole body spinning in the air so many times it's impossible to count the revolutions. I dodge and his foot misses my head by a millimeter. He lands gracefully on the other side of me.

"Teach me how to do that." I'm in awe of his strength and agility.

"We need to find somewhere to train with more height." He jumps up to the ceiling. "It's not safe to do aerial training down here. Shit. Rock's head nearly touches this ceiling *without* jumping."

"No it doesn't." The ceiling is at least ten feet, high for a basement, but my instinct to defend Rock's home overtook my reason. Gray is right.

"I wonder how high I can jump now." I bounce up to touch the ceiling. My palms land flat, and my arms were unprepared. I nearly smash my head into the concrete.

Landing, I turn toward Gray. "Wow. I didn't even bend my knees! That felt as easy as raising onto my toes."

"You haven't even begun to tap into your potential." Gray stands casually a few feet away, but I sense tension in his body and know from experience that he might challenge me with another attack at any second. But not the kind of attack my body craves.

I circle around him, planning a possible strike of my own. "You keep claiming I've got so much potential, but how do you know?"

He dives over me, his body stretching along the ceiling. He twists before landing and pins me from behind, fangs at my neck. The heat of his breath refuels my desire.

Desire to feed from him, to have him feed from me—and the overwhelming but unmistakable desire to feel him thrusting inside me.

He lets me go. "Let's sit. There are some things you need to know. Might as well tell you a few secrets, now it's just us vamps."

We cross to the end of the room and he settles down on a mat there, leaning against the stone wall.

I slide down the wall beside him.

As much as I thirst for Gray, I also thirst for knowledge. I want to learn all the things my Maker should have taught me.

"How often do I need to feed?" I ask. "How often from humans and how often from... from you?" Oh, how I'd love to take his vein again, have him take mine.

"Depends. Everyone's different. As you grow more powerful you'll need human blood less often. Do you think you'll need to feed tonight?"

I shake my head, then I curl toward him. "I don't need human blood, but can I drink from *you* again?"

His pupils dilate, and his chest rises with a long inhale, as if his memories of that night are as fantastic as mine.

He shifts a few inches away. "None of that, princess. It's lesson time."

"Okay, teacher. Where do we start?" I slide my hand toward the fabric of his sweat pants that fit his body like they were tailor made for his athletic but slender body. Even when working out, Gray looks elegant.

He pushes back his hair, but a lock falls down across his eyes. I can smell his blood, almost taste it on my tongue. I sit on my hands to keep myself from touching him.

"Why don't you ask me some questions," he says somewhat hoarsely. "Then we'll go from there."

"How old were you when you were turned?" Gray seems young—and so hot.

He raises his eyebrows. "I meant ask me general questions about vampire culture, but okay. We can start there. I was twenty-four."

"I was twenty-two! We're basically the same age."

He smiles and his teeth scrape his lower lip. I can tell what he's thinking or at least what *part* of him is thinking. As much as he tries to hide it, Gray wants me as badly as I want him. If he weren't such a gentleman we'd be rolling around on this mat.

I look down, ashamed to keep thinking of Grayson in a sexual way when Rock's the one I love. But the big man rejected me and refuses to even discuss it further.

"Who made you?" I ask. "Astrid said it was one of the Ancients. What does that even mean?"

He settles back against the wall, his eyes going someplace else for a moment, somewhere painful, and I pull one of my hands out from under my thigh to touch his fingers gently.

At my touch, he turns toward me with a sad smile. But he pulls his hand away from mine.

"The Ancients is the name given to the original vampires."

"From Transylvania?"

He laughs. "No. The Middle East and northern Africa. From the places Western historians call the cradle of civilization."

"And you were made by one of the first ones?"

He nods.

I suck in a sharp breath, imagining how many centuries, perhaps millennia, Gray must have lived. How much he's experienced. No wonder he calls me a baby.

"How...how was the first vampire made?" From what little I know about human to vampire transitions, it seems like a chicken and egg problem.

"No one knows for certain," he says. "My Maker taught me that the original vampires were a product of evolution, like any other living thing on Earth." He shrugs. "But vampires remain rare."

"Why?"

"The process to create progeny is complicated and risky. Only the most powerful vampires are able to complete it without killing themselves or the human they are hoping to turn."

A million questions run through my mind. "If it's so difficult, then how do I exist?"

"A mystery for the ages."

I frown. "And my Maker must have been very powerful."

He shrugs. "Another mystery." He looks at me intently, as if he's looking for something specific. Then he pulls his gaze away. "And there's another reason vampires are rare."

"Why?"

"Because it's so difficult to procreate."

"To make babies?"

He nods. "It doesn't happen often. Vampire couples have a one in a hundred chance of conceiving once every hundred years."

I try to get my head around that number. "So even if a vampire couple is together for hundreds of years..."

"They might never have children."

"That's sad."

"Some think so. Me?" He shoots me a mischievous smile. "I like to take full advantage of unlimited, consequence-free shagging."

My blood heats with desire and jealousy at the idea of Gray having sex with so many partners. "How many?" I ask softly.

"How many what?"

I fiddle with my leggings, tugging on the fabric over my thigh and letting it snap back. "How many women."

"How many women have I...shagged? Is that what you want to know?" His tone is mocking.

Biting my lower lip, I nod.

"You jealous, princess?"

"What if I am?" Gathering my courage, I arch, pushing forward my chest and moving toward him a few inches.

His eyes darken in response, his pupils widening with obvious desire. Again, I'm equal parts glad and frustrated that he's restraining himself, not doing what he so obviously wants. My body wants him so badly, even if my heart wants Rock.

Gray maintains eye contact, but his expression softens. "I've had my fair share."

"But you've never taken a mate?'

He shakes his head. "Don't see the point of tying myself down."

"Can vampires have children with...with non-vampires?" I wonder about me and Rock and how badly I want to spend my life with him. Could we raise a child together some day?

"There are rumors of interspecies conception, but most think it's rubbish." His posture makes me think he's holding something back. But then he shakes his finger at me. "You, young lady, have completely changed the subject."

"What was the subject?"

"You asked me about your potential. How I know you have more. The night we met..." Licking his lower lip, he draws a long breath. "When you drank from me..." He lifts my hand from the mat where I'd slid it dangerously close to his leg and sets it down on my own thigh, shaking his head like I'm naughty.

"What about it?" My heart rate quickens, remembering the powerful feelings I had that night and wanting to feel that way again.

"I've never experienced anything like that before," he says.

My cheeks heat, remembering my reaction to the taste of his blood, how I almost rubbed through our clothing, humping him on that couch. "Astrid said what happened between us was normal."

He shakes his head. "There was nothing normal about that. In fact, there's nothing normal about you."

"Gee, way to make a girl feel great about herself." He's made me feel like a horny teenager, and I suppose that in many ways I am.

"Your differences are nothing to be ashamed of, princess."

"You just said I'm not normal."

"But that's a *good* thing. Or at least an *interesting* thing." He turns slightly toward me, bending the long leg closest to my body so that his knee comes within millimeters of touching mine. "When you drank from me, the effect it had..." He sucks in a breath.

"I could tell." I look at his crotch. "And I can tell now." My breathing accelerates.

"Yes, that." He chuckles, slowly shaking his head. "But my woody isn't what I mean. What you made me feel. Princess, it was far more than a hard cock." He brushes his hand over his package, and his breath catches.

My heart pounds. "What do you mean?"

"What was extraordinary that night was the power transfer. I haven't felt anything like it. Certainly not when someone was taking *my* blood. Never."

"Power transfer?"

"Yes." He looks at me quizzically. "Malcolm and Astrid must have told you about that. No?" He shakes his head. "Vampires need human blood for food, but we also need to feed from each other. Vampire-to-vampire feedings are less about food and more about sharing."

"Sharing what?"

"Power and..."

"And what?"

"Power and... Power is the main thing."

Clearly there's something else he doesn't want to say.

"And you shared some of your...your *power* with me?" I ask. That explains why I've felt stronger ever since. Like I could jump twenty feet in the air without effort. My newfound strength isn't just from the physical training. It's more than that. Some of the power came from Gray, and I like that.

"That's what I mean about your potential." He brushes back his hair. "As a baby—"

"Please don't call me that. You know I'm not a baby."

"Okay, *princess*." He winks.

I slap his chest lightly, and he moves his hands over the spot, grimacing as if I actually injured him. Then his face turns serious and he drops his hands down. "Joking aside, as a—as a *recently made* vampire, one who'd never fed from another vampire, not even her Maker—" He shakes his head. "Assuming that's true."

"It is."

"Given that, then you *never* should have been able to draw from me like that, with so much power, to feast from me as if..." He looks away.

"As if what?"

He shakes his head, refusing to look at me.

I touch his forearm lightly. "Please, Gray. Tell me. How else am I going to learn?"

"You fed from me like you were my mate. Like you needed my blood to survive." He turns away from me. "And it made me so sodding hungry."

"Hungry?" I ask softly, my blood coursing wildly in my veins.

His blood is pumping hard, too. I can hear it, I can smell it, almost taste it. I run my tongue over my teeth, my fangs pulsing with need. "Hungry for what?"

"For you, princess." The words come out low and hard as he turns toward me. "Ever since that night, I've wanted to *consume* you, to take you in every way I can imagine."

"Then take me," I whisper, barely hearing myself over the blood rushing hard in my ears. "Take me however you want, Gray. Because I can't even describe how much I want you."

In a flash, I'm on my back on the mat.

His long body presses against mine, and his lips devour me in a ferocious kiss that turns my body to liquid fire. I'm molten lava, lava that's consuming him too. Gray is part of me now, our bodies uniting.

His hand slides between my T-shirt and sports bra and squeezes, then he pushes up the fabric of the latter, forcing the rows of tight elastic over my breast. His fingers graze my nipple, lightly teasing and then tightening over the hardened bud.

I groan into his mouth as a shot of pleasure transfers directly from my nipple to my sex.

Holding his head, I change the angle of our kiss, wanting to drag his entire body in through my mouth, feeling like I can. Yet still I want more... So much more...

Breaking the kiss, I press my lips against his neck. His vein throbs under my tongue, and I lick. My fangs graze his skin, my anticipation of the meal almost as good as the real thing.

I'm beyond tempted to bite, but my instincts say I should ask his permission—and right now I've got other priorities.

Kissing him again, I drape one leg over his butt and stroke the mounds of muscle with my calf. He shifts between my legs, his hardness stroking me through our clothes, through far too many layers of fabric. I tug down on his sweat pants.

He pulls away from my lips, supporting himself on his arms as he arches to press even harder against me. He strokes his erection against me, thrusting his hips as he looks down into my eyes.

"Are you sure about this, princess?"

I nod, even as an image of Rock flashes in my mind, bringing guilt.

Gray tweaks my nipple. I buck, and my sex presses up against his hard length. I gasp. "Please. Yes. Gray. I've never—"

He stops suddenly, his body freezing above mine. "Never what?"

I don't answer.

"You're a virgin?"

"Yes. No." I shake my head, angry with myself for throwing ice water on the scene. "Okay. What I mean is, in the way that matters—that matters to me. Yes, I am a virgin." I close my eyes for a long blink as the concern in his eyes becomes too much to bear.

I need to explain. "My body...it's been penetrated more times than I can count, before and after I transitioned. I've been violated, abused."

He pulls back, remaining above me, hand over my breast, but his erection is no longer digging against my sex.

I want that delicious pressure back, but I also want him to understand why sharing this act with him, sharing the act with passion, instead of hate or malice, is so important to me.

"Technically, I'm not a virgin, Gray. But I've never made love, I've never had *consensual* sex." Is that true after what happened with Rock? "I've never consensually had a man's penis inside me."

The only thing that's ever entered me with consent was Rock's tongue, and remembering that feeling sends lust rippling through me.

"And you want me to..." His thumb flicks my hardened nipple.

My back arches, and his erection grazes my body. His muscles tighten, his shoulders and biceps visibly changing above me, growing, hardening.

It's the hottest thing I've ever seen.

"Yes, I want you," I cry out. "I want you very much." I want to do this with Rock, but he won't. And even if Rock wanted to have sex with me, given his size, perhaps it's best if he's not my first consensual partner.

Gray stares into my eyes as if making a decision, then he bends down to kiss me, more tenderly this time.

Slowly, he nibbles my mouth, tugging at my lower lip, then pulling my tongue between his lips, between his teeth. The kissing is delicious and erotic and tender, and new fires light inside me. I've never wanted anything this badly, and yet nerves stir inside me.

Breaking our kiss, he rises to his knees and straddles one of my thighs. Slowly he removes his shirt.

Once it's revealed, I gasp at the beauty of Gray's chest—smooth except for some dark hair in the center, his skin smooth and tanned. He isn't nearly as big as Rock, but he's all male. Gray's chest is strong, and his abs are like ridges sculpted into the beach by strong waves.

I reach up to touch him, to trace my fingers down the middle of his chest and over the wave-like shape of his abs, and as my fingers explore, his breaths become ragged and audible. His erection strains against his sweat pants.

Standing quickly, he drags off his pants to reveal red underwear that leaves nothing to my imagination. His erection's thicker than I expected, and much longer, and it bounces straight up against his belly when he draws down the briefs and tosses them to the side.

Even Gray's cock is long and elegant.

I pull off my shirt, wanting to feel his skin against mine while we do this, then I struggle with the sports bra.

While the stretchy fabric is caught over my face, Gray drags down my leggings, removing them in one fluid motion, and I finally free my body from the bra's entrapment.

Kneeling, he slides his hands up my legs, and his gaze rises to meet mine. The combination of utter lust and admiration I see in his eyes nearly slays me. Men have always found me attractive—it's not hard to tell—but I've never had a man look at me like this. Like I'm a work of art and a meal all at once.

I lift my hips, and he drags down my panties, sliding them over my ankles and toes. When they're off he leans forward, slowly at first, then he nearly dives onto me as he captures my lips. As we kiss, our hands explore each other's bodies, and his hard rod throbs against my belly. Every skin cell it touches welcomes the pressure and friction with delight.

He breaks the kiss. "You're sure this is what you want?"

I nod.

"I need to hear it, princess. It's natural for vampires to have strong sexual drives, but after what you've told me—" He shakes his head. "I need to be sure that you want this."

"Yes. Please. Now." I spread my legs on the mat, looking up into his eyes.

Will sex feel different, less painful, when the penetration's invited? I brace for the intrusion, but instead of plunging, he bends to kiss me again as he slides his fingers through my folds. The feeling's delicious, but it's not what I crave and I squirm with impatience.

But I soon forget my urgency, absorbed instead by his long lean fingers that are tracing my folds and circling my opening as his tongue strokes against mine, mimicking what I want him to do between my legs.

His finger presses inside me, and I gasp against his mouth.

"You okay?"

I kiss him in response, pulling his tongue hard into my mouth and sucking.

He growls deep in his throat and starts to move his finger inside me. His digit isn't as thick as Rock's tongue, but it's longer and hits places Rock didn't. It makes me want more. Need more.

He breaks our kiss and I go for his neck.

He pulls away, shaking his head. "Not a good idea, princess."

"Why not?"

He brushes back my hair, then cradles my head with his forearm. "This will be too much if we feed. Trust me. Better if we wait to feed during sex. Okay?"

I nod. Warmth rises inside me as his words confirm that a next time is on the table, when we haven't even completed the act a first time.

His finger withdraws, and I soon feel the press of something else, something hard and soft at the same time. Something much thicker than his finger.

"Ready?" he asks.

"Very." My answer is certain, yet nerves invade. I don't want to associate this act, or this man, with the abuse that I've suffered. I want this to be something new, something wonderful. Have I set my hopes too high?

Guiding his erection with one hand, he pushes his hips forward, and with a sudden sharp thrust he's inside me.

I sense he isn't deep, but the burst of pain, more like discomfort, radiates from the point of impact and then morphs into pleasure. My sex floods with desire.

Looking into my eyes, he remains still, and I like the feeling of his body inside mine, the fullness and the ultimate intimacy of even his shallow intrusion. And I love the concern in his expression, mixed with obvious restraint as veins rise on his temples and his breathing rate increases.

His hand slides from his penis onto my belly and then he slowly presses his hips forward, pushing into me farther.

I gasp, my mouth dropping open.

"You okay?"

I nod. "I'll tell you if it's not. I promise."

He strokes my belly, then up between my breasts as he pushes farther in, slowly, moving millimeter by millimeter, until I can't imagine him reaching any deeper. Lodged inside me, he stays still for a moment.

My insides tighten around him, then he pulls back just as leisurely as he went in, moving unbearably slowly until he's nearly out. The sensations are better than I ever could have imagined.

He repeats this motion again, and then again and again, slowly pushing in and out of me as he continues to stroke my belly and chest with his hand, and it's good. So good. Finally I've had sex that feels good.

Gray looks down into my eyes with so much tenderness and concern. It's amazing and makes my heart fill with gratitude. But while this ultra-tender act is pleasurable—so pleasurable—I start to long for the lust, the hunger, the need, the kind of sex I saw at the club.

I lift my hips to meet his next stroke.

Sinking deeper, he gasps, his eyelids closing slightly. He holds still inside me as my body adjusts to the deeper penetration, yielding to him, and even more pleasure points awaken. Sliding his hand under one of my thighs, he lifts it to bend my knee, and my foot slides onto his back.

Repositioned, he rocks into me, slowly at first but with a strong rhythm, going deeper and faster as he continues. And I love it, I love each heightening moment of it, but still I want more.

His hand slides down over my belly, and his thumb quickly finds my clit. He circles there matching the speed of his accelerating thrusts.

My insides catch fire.

“Gray,” I moan his name.

“Princess,” he growls.

I don’t mind the nickname in that tone of voice, and I feel an orgasm building inside me. As if he senses it, too, he increases his speed along with the pressure on my clit.

I arch against him as my climax takes hold and my insides squeeze around his hardness, pulsing while the rest of me shakes with rippling pleasure.

When it subsides, he strokes the side of my face. “And how was that?”

“Fantastic.”

“I’m glad.” He kisses my nose softly, and then slides out of my body, hissing slightly as his erection strikes my thigh.

“You’re still hard,” I say with surprise.

“That, princess, was not for me.” He kisses me, and the kiss is so delicious I almost get distracted, but my lust isn’t sated, and clearly neither is his.

“Take me again, Gray.”

He rises up to look hungrily into my eyes.

“Take me harder, take me however you need for *your* pleasure this time.”

“That was plenty of pleasure, princess.” He kneels between my legs, bending over me and stroking my face.

“You sure about that?” I take hold of his damp hardness.

He groans and his hips thrust forward sharply, sliding against my palm.

“You’re not too sore?” he asks.

“Not a bit.” It’s not true, but I love the ache that I feel, an ache that makes me crave more.

“Because sex between vampires...” He whistles between closed lips. “It can get intense, some might say violent.”

“That’s what I want.” I witnessed passionate, hard sex

in the club the other night, not to mention at Xavier's court. And I want that. But consensually. I want to participate in the sex act, not have things done to me.

I want sex that's not about torture or control. What Gray and I just did gave me pleasure, but I sense that there's more, that the experience will be even more powerful if Gray seeks his own pleasure too, and the idea of sharing pleasure with Gray, doing for him what he did for me...

"I want you to fuck me," I plead. "Really fuck me. Fuck me hard. I want it more than anything. Please."

Spreading my thighs with his legs, he tugs me down on the mat and then presses my knees toward my chest, opening my sex wide to him. With my legs trapped at my sides, he enters me, landing inside deep and hard with one unyielding plunge.

Partially recovered already, I gasp at the sharp pain of the penetration, and before I have a chance to adjust, his hips begin to thrust.

I moan, loving how he fills me, how he moves above me, his muscles flexing, his expression growing darker with lust. This—this deep, hard penetration is what I was craving, what my body knew it wanted even if it had never felt it with pleasure.

My breaths synchronize with his thrusts, my pelvis rising to draw him in more deeply. Each hard stroke brings slight pain when he hits my channel's limit, but it's hard to differentiate that from all the pleasure. Like the pain is soothing an even deeper ache.

Our eyes make contact and my breath catches in my chest. There's nothing else in the room anymore, nothing in the world, nothing exists but the universe I see in Gray's eyes. His eyes swallow me whole, draw me down into a deep cave where it's dark and light at the same time, where I'm safe and no one can ever find or hurt me.

I'd be happy if this went on forever, if we spent the rest of our lives joined this way, moving together with power and passion. Just like this.

But he shifts, tucks my legs over his shoulders and moves his hands to the mat.

I can no longer see his face. I'm sandwiched now, folded under him and unable to move at all as his pumping accelerates. Each thrust goes even deeper and strikes places he didn't reach earlier. Friction from his speed heats my insides and he's so deep his balls slap against me, the wet sounds of our act heightening my desire, exciting me as his cock pounds inside me.

I love this too. I love it. I love every part of it. But still, I want more. I want to move. I want to be a more active participant.

As if reading my mind, he pulls out, then guides me onto my hands and knees, pulling my hips back and running his fingers through my burning, wet folds.

"From behind, it will feel even deeper, princess. Stop me if it hurts."

Looking back over my shoulder I assure him with my eyes and watch his expression change as he pushes inside me, and I love the strain and intense pleasure so obvious on his face as I squeeze around him.

One hand on my shoulder, one on my hip, he drives again, pulling me back against him, and I rock, shifting back and forth on my knees, using my newfound power as we find our rhythm together, my body increasing the force of each of his thrusts, so powerful and deep.

Each time he lands deeply, I cry out, and each strike

brings more pleasure than the last until I feel sure I'll explode from the ecstasy.

"Ready?" he asks, and I wonder what could possibly be next. I've finally reached a point where I'm not craving more.

But after his question, his speed really takes off. He moves, we both move, at the pace of a thoroughbred race-horse—no, a cheetah, faster than a cheetah. He drives so quickly I know the human eye would barely be able to detect what's happening between us; it's so fast the friction between us ignites. I feel sure we're on fire.

I cry out, my back undulating as I meet each thrust, my body moving in ways I had no idea it could. In ways it knows only by instinct.

He pulls out and I gasp. Then, in one fluid motion, he lifts me up off the mat as he stands. He turns me to face him and pins me against the wall with his body as he impales me again on his cock. I wrap my legs around him as he slams into me so hard and so fast I worry we're shaking the building's foundations, that an earthquake will register.

I hold onto his shoulders as he pounds. My fangs are so close to his neck. His vein is so tempting. I lick his throat.

With a shouting exhale, he pulls out, sets me down and turns me to face away from him, pressing my body against the wall. Then, without warning, he drives into me again, the force lifting my feet off the floor and pressing the length of my body into the wall as he pounds. The skin on my lower belly rubs until I wonder if he can feel the stones through my flesh.

He tugs my hips from the wall and I press my hands against the stone and arch my back, changing the angle and increasing the depth. His finger lands on my clit.

With each hard pulsing stroke, his finger rubs the overly sensitive bud, and I put my hand under my face to shield it from the stone and to stifle my screams of pleasure as my body convulses in an orgasm so intense—so different from the ones before it—I can't even compare. My entire body takes part in this climax, every muscle and nerve joining together in spasms of pleasure.

"I'm going to come," he shouts. "Fuck, princess, the things you do to me."

It doesn't seem like I'm doing much of anything, but his speed increases again, his hands tightening on my hips, and his thrusts grow more erratic, more forceful, more deep.

He groans and I'm still having aftershocks from my orgasm as his seed explodes inside me.

My horrid stepfather ejaculated inside me many times. I knew it from the sticky evidence after, but this... It must be my vampiric senses heightened by arousal, because I feel the power of each eruption, feel the heat and force of his thick fluid spraying inside me.

He slows, still moving, but now at a more human-like pace, and then he withdraws, turning me and pulling me tightly into his arms. "Holy fuck, princess."

"Exactly what I was about to say." I kiss his chest, licking his skin, as he cups my ass with his hands, caressing me gently, rubbing our hot bodies together as we both come down from the high.

"Is sex always like that?" I ask when I'm capable.

"No." His fingers trail up and down my back. "No, princess. *That* was special. Very fucking special."

He lifts his head, looking over mine.

He pushes back from me.

"What is it?" I ask, startled.

He gestures behind me with his eyes, then drops his

head forward, shaking it from side to side as if he suddenly regrets everything we've done.

I turn around.

My stomach contracts. Shame and regret replace every ounce of my satiated pleasure.

"Rock." I take a step toward him.

CHAPTER TWENTY

Selina

I stand frozen.

Rock remains in the corner of the room, quiet, not moving, and I realize with horror that he isn't standing right at the door. He didn't just walk in. How much did he see?

Something brushes my shoulder and I look down to see that Gray has draped my T-shirt over my body. He presses a kiss against the top of my head, and then I scramble to dress as he strides, already fully clothed, toward Rock.

Which one of them will win in a fight? Which one will die? Rock is so much larger, and part giant, but Gray is a vampire.

But instead of attacking, they talk, then shake hands. I try to hear what they're saying, but my blood's too loud in my ears. I pull up my leggings, my legs shaking, my sex throbbing and my mouth unbearably dry.

What time is it? I feel the need to feed, after all.

Does sex fuel vampire hunger? No way can I ask Gray

the question. Not right now. Not in front of Rock. I could call Astrid. But then I'll have to admit to her what I did. That I cheated on Rock.

Rock claps Gray on the back, and then the vampire leaves the room, leaving me alone with Rock. I'm so confused.

What the hell could they have said to each other?

Legs like jelly, I walk slowly forward and we meet in the middle of the room. I stare at the floor, shaking, unable to look him in the eyes. "I'm sorry, Rock. It just... It just happened. I'm so sorry."

Using his bent index finger, he lifts my chin, and I reluctantly look into his eyes. Rock doesn't look angry or even sad. He looks calm and happy.

And that hurts.

He doesn't seem to care that he just found me having sex with someone else. When he said he didn't love me, he meant it. He doesn't care—not at all.

"It's okay, Selina," he says softly. "It makes me happy that you've found someone to satisfy...that you and Grayson... It's okay."

I step back, shaking my head. "No, it's not okay. It's not okay with *me,* and it kills me to hear you say that it's okay with you."

He tips his head to the side, a question in his eyes. "What's wrong? Did Grayson hurt you? Force you? It did seem very...very rigorous."

My chest nearly caves with shame, but it quickly turns to wounded anger. "How can you be so calm about this? So cold? So unfeeling?"

He looks at me intently. "Believe me, although I am calm, I am far from 'cold' or 'unfeeling' on this subject. Your happiness is very important to me."

"So." I shake my head. "Are you saying it's okay if I go around fucking every man that I see? In front of you?"

He frowns. "Not every man, no. But whether he admits it or not, Grayson cares for you, Acushla."

"Don't call me that."

His head snaps back like I punched him.

"Do not call me that, again," I repeat. "Not if you don't mean it."

"I do mean it." He pulls me into his arms, enveloping my body completely.

I warm against him, his arms like a comforting blanket around me. But his holding me isn't enough. It will never be enough.

"Rock, you don't understand." I push back on his chest so I can see into his eyes. "I'm falling in love with you." I look down. "I might have already fallen, and I don't mind saying it, even though you don't love me back."

"But I do." He holds my face in his hands, forcing my gaze up to his. "I love you, pulse of my heart. I love you with the power of a raging river. I love you like no other before you. I love you heart of my heart."

Blood pounds so loud in my ears I'm not sure that I heard him or if I dreamed it; I'm not sure that the words weren't carried to my ears through the wishes of my pounding blood.

His bloodstream's loud, too, his two hearts pumping with unfathomable force. Did I really hear what he said?

"I betrayed you, Rock. I made love to another man, and it breaks my heart that you don't even care."

He presses a kiss against my forehead, a kiss so hard and long I feel it might brand me. "I love you," he says. "And I'll love you forever. I will worship you, and if you'll let me I will protect you and defend you against any threat or foe."

"Rock." My voice comes out in a whisper, a shadow of itself.

And then he takes my face in his hands and kisses me, and soon our lips are devouring each other's with so much passion I feel like I'm floating. And then I realize I *am* floating, or at least my feet are no longer on the floor, my body effortlessly held aloft by Rock, my big strong giant who loves me, loves me as I love him, but...

I break the kiss. "What you saw. Gray and me. It didn't make you jealous?"

Rock shakes his head. "It made me happy. Happy for you. Happy that you've found someone who can fulfill a need for you that I can't. Malcolm trusts Grayson, and from what I've seen this week he's a good man. I like him." He says this earnestly, not a hint of deceit in his voice, but his eyes still seem a little sad.

I struggle with my feelings. One part of me wants Rock to love me so much that he'd crush any rival, but the thought of his hurting Gray or asking me never to see him again makes me ill.

I realize in that moment that losing Gray would break my heart too. My insides are still pulsing with the memory of his cock inside me. And I want him inside me again. I need Gray. I can't sort out my emotions, but I know that my body longs for more Gray. And it's not just my body; he's touched my heart too.

Can I love more than one man? Or can I love one man and have sex with another?

Red lights flash in the four corners of the room.

Rock's body stiffens. His body is always hard, just like his name suggests—even when he's sleeping—but when he tenses like this... I run my hand down the hard ridge at the side of his neck.

"What's wrong?"

"Police," he says. "Upstairs in the bar. Come. Let's get you safely downstairs."

Selina

I PACE inside Rock's apartment, terrified about what could be happening upstairs. If the police arrived before Gray left the building, or if they caught him on the way out... Is Gray already dead?

I bend forward, the mere idea like a stake to my heart. My chest heaves as I fight off the unbearable pain.

The highs and lows of this day have been exhausting, what I imagine a roller coaster must feel like—something else I never got to try before turning, and now never will unless someplace runs them at night.

As I circle the room for the umpteenth time, one of the paintings distracts me from my fear. Bold slashes of color crisscross the canvas in lavender, pale green, soft gray. Feathery, finer strokes swirl over top, and... I step closer. There's another layer in between, one that looks like a veil, like it's forcing the viewer to see portions of the bold strokes through a soft-focused lens.

And as I stare at the image, it's like some of the shapes start to move. The top layer of swirls and strokes slide over the filmy layer, dancing and skipping, hiding and revealing the bold swaths of color beneath.

I blink, and the image stills, but every moment I look at this painting I see something different, the fine strokes of paint on top now seem sensual, like they're luxuriating in the touch of the thin veil underneath. And the bold strokes exude so much force and power.

When I was homeless and human, I'd go to the big art gallery on Dundas on the nights it was free, and I often visited commercial galleries, even when the snotty, well-dressed staff working there made it clear I wasn't welcome.

And at the library, I've seen images of some of the most famous paintings hung in museums around the world. While I know paintings are often very different in real life versus a computer screen or book, I've seen more works of art than most people my age, and I've never seen anything like this.

A feeling of peace washes over me. My terror about the police presence upstairs doesn't disappear, but there's no sense letting the worry overwhelm me. There's nothing I can do.

And there's nothing I can do to take back what Gray and I did, or that Rock saw us.

I can't sort out my feelings for Gray, except to know that there's something beyond the sexual fire, but looking at this painting, I can convince myself that it's going to be okay, that I'm looking for problems where there are none.

I didn't sense any animosity between Rock and Gray, and if neither man is bothered, why should I be?

They shook hands; they man-hugged. And Rock...Rock told me he loved me. His confession is still sinking in and fills me with joy.

Rock and I are in love. I draw long, luxurious breaths as I let the idea absorb. Why did I let fear overstep my comprehending or responding to the most beautiful words ever?

Can I really love Rock and *make love* with Gray? Feed from Gray? Have him feed from me? Gray said I drank from him like I was his mate. What did he mean?

"You like that one?" Rock asks.

I turn, shocked that I didn't hear him come down. I nod, a lump of emotion blocking my throat.

"Is everything okay upstairs?" I choke out.

"Yup. All clear. Seems they were just doing a regular check. The cops handed their cards to Kev and Chelle. One to me." Shaking his head, he grins. "Bad news for you, though."

"What's that?"

He pulls a card from his pocket, flipping it back and forth between his index and middle finger. "Constable Colton Young. Guess this card makes me his deputy or something."

"What?" I laugh as he steps toward me.

"I'm a spy for the cops now. At least, an undercover informant, charged to report any individuals 'exhibiting suspicious, vampire-like behaviors.'" He makes air quotes as he repeats what I assume are the cop's words.

Hand on my butt, Rock pulls me hard against him. "Seen anyone suspicious around here, miss? Any vampire-like behaviors?"

My body undulates, loving how it feels to have his huge hands on my ass, his thighs against my belly. "No officer. Honest. Haven't seen any vampires around here."

"Are you sure, miss?" Bending me back, he slides his nose along my neck, inhaling deeply. "Because I'm not sure what I'm sensing here, but something smells fishy."

"Fishy?" I mock punch him, and he starts to laugh, his huge body shaking mine as he returns me to an upright position.

"Not fishy. Sorry. I hit my role-play limits. Never was much of a performer." His voice drops with that last line.

Did Rock want to be an actor at some point? He did

mention a circus. There's so much I have yet to discover about my man, and I can't wait to start finding out.

"Where did you get this painting?" I ask, turning back toward it. "Who's the artist?"

"Artist?" His hand wraps around me from behind and he strokes my ribs. "That's going a bit far, don't you think?"

"So, it's no one famous, then?" I lean forward to check again for a signature. "I mean, to me this is a museum-level piece, but nothing like I've seen before. The artist has a style of their own."

"How do you know so much about art?" he asks.

"It's what I studied. Well, I don't have a degree or anything, but I audited some courses, read tons of books and studied on the Internet. I would have given anything to take art history for real. When I was human, I actually landed a job doing graphic design at a small ad agency."

"You sound sad when you say that." He kisses my head.

"I got the job just before I was turned. I was looking forward to the job more than anything, but I couldn't take it."

"Why not?"

"Because of, you know, *daylight*?"

"Acushla, you've got an eternity to make your dreams come true. So what if that employer insisted you work during the day. You can find someone who'll let you work from home, or at night."

"Do you really think so?"

"I know so."

"But won't they suspect?"

"There are plenty of vampire-friendly workplaces. You just have to know where to look. Malcolm and Astrid—not to mention Gray—can help you with that. I'll bet they even have graphic artists working at FJS."

My heart swells, my emotional roller coaster is back on an uptick again, or is it a descent? I'm on whichever is the best part.

Standing here with Rock, looking at his beautiful painting, I feel utterly safe and content. "I really do love this painting."

"That's because it looks like you."

"What?" I turn toward him, then back to the painting.

"Graceful and strong, delicate and bold, it captures you perfectly."

I smile. "And you really don't know who the artist is?"

"Oh, I know."

"Who is it?"

"Me." He shrugs. "I painted all of these." He gestures around the room.

I gasp, my gaze darting around the room over all of the striking artwork then back to Rock. "Are you pulling my leg?"

Shaking his head, he rubs his head, leaving a few of the blond curls on top standing up from the crowd.

"Rock. You're very talented. These are amazing." My love grows, expands beyond the limit I already thought was the max.

His cheeks flush with embarrassed pride, then he turns back to the painting I was staring at.

"You know," he says softly, "when I did this one, I think I was painting you."

"What do you mean?" I lean my head against his chest. "I remember seeing it the first time I came down to your apartment."

"I painted it fifty years ago—fifty-seven years ago, to be exact."

"Then, what do you mean?"

He turns to face me, one hand cupping my head as the other arm rests heavily on my shoulder. "When I painted this, I think I knew, deep inside...I must have known through my loneliness and despair, that someday I would find you."

My heart swells. "But I wasn't even born yet." My mom wasn't born yet.

He shakes his head and presses his hand over his heart. "Not physically, no. But in here." He taps his chest. "In my heart, I already knew the promise of you, and that promise pulled me through, kept me going when there was so little to make me think life was worth living."

"Oh, Rock." My heart nearly shatters from the combination of love and the desire to sooth all his pain—past and present.

I trace my hand down the side of his face, loving how his pale whiskers scrape my palm and how his eyelashes flutter as if my touch is the most fabulous thing he's ever felt. "I love you so much."

"I love you, too, Acushla. I love you so much."

He bends and his lips capture mine.

CHAPTER
TWENTY-ONE

Rock

With Selina in my arms, her lips kissing mine, her hands on my body, it's easy to believe I could be happy. That I could lead a normal life. That we could love each other, build a life together. But I know it's not possible.

Pleasure purrs from inside her as she strokes her tongue along mine, and mine strokes hers right back.

I pull my hips away from her soft body as my constrained rod hardens at the memory of having my tongue between her legs, drinking her in. If we did that ten times a day it wouldn't be enough. And while I watched the tall vampire fuck my love, a yearning grew like a painful lump inside me. Pain I can live with, and her obvious pleasure cushioned my pain.

I would love to be the man who could give her that pleasure, fulfill her primal need, but that's not possible, and her happiness is more important than anything else.

I did my best to reassure Grayson, to make sure he knew he was welcome as far as I was concerned. Welcome to continue her training and making love to her—if that's what she wants and needs.

I hope he believed me. If Gray can satisfy my love's sexual desires, then she'll stop pressing me, and it might help assuage my guilt.

Her hand brushes over the front of my jeans.

Fighting a moan, I sweep her into my arms to hold her aloft. Her arms circle my neck, where they're less dangerous, and her fingers play with the hairs at the back of my head and thread through the curls on top as we kiss. Her body writhes in my arms, her breasts rubbing against me, her pelvis circling. So fucking sexy.

"Rock." She pulls away from my lips, panting. "Make love to me. Please."

I shake my head.

Pain invades her eyes.

If she weren't a vampire I'm sure there'd be tears in her eyes right now, and I hate that I'm the cause. I want to make her understand, but if she knew the truth, what I've done to so many women, her love for me would vanish.

No woman could ever love a man who's hurt so many, especially not a woman who's been assaulted herself.

"Why?" She casts her eyes down. "I wish you hadn't seen what happened between me and Gray. I'm so sorry." She looks back into my eyes, the pain and uncertainty in hers like daggers to my heart. "Is that why you won't have sex with me? Because I did it with Grayson?"

I shake my head.

"Then why?" She hits my chest lightly. "I'm not some little girl, you know. Even though you may have been on this Earth a hundred years longer than me, I'm an adult. I know what I want and it's insulting for you to treat me like a child."

"That's not it. Acushla..."

"Please, Rock." Her hip rubs against my ribs, and she squirms, wiggling and pushing against me, clearly trying to move lower on my body or to get me to set her down so she can touch me down there.

"Stop it, Selina." I set her down and quickly back away.

Her chest heaves, and her eyes fill with questions as she steps toward me.

I step away. "No."

Her head snaps back, her hands land over her ears, and the glasses in my cupboards rattle.

I realize that I yelled. Except for that night when Selina was in danger from those cops, I haven't raised my voice in decades. They might have heard me two stories up, but I don't regret it.

The volume of my voice convinced her. Or at least it stopped her for the moment. She drops her hands off her ears.

"Why don't you want me?" she asks quietly. "What's wrong with me?"

I shake my head slowly, the pain of hurting her slicing through my chest. "Nothing. Selina. There is absolutely nothing wrong with you. This is all about me."

"Then tell me. Please." She takes a small step forward, but when I tense, she stops. "I love you, Rock. Whatever it is, you can tell me."

I wish more than anything that were true. I have to tell her something, even if it isn't the whole truth. Her pain is so palpable it might crush me.

"Let's sit." I drop into a chair and she slowly moves to the sofa and curls up in the corner.

"Sex..." I shake my head. "I know that you've had terrible experiences, and I'm glad that you're healing from that. Truly happy. But for me..." How can I explain this without telling her what I've done? "For me, even the *idea* of sex is repulsive."

She gasps, backing into the seat cushions, clearly hurt.

"Not sex with you." I shake my head. "Sex with *anyone*. In the past..." I close my eyes for a moment. "My species, whatever I am. We aren't made to have sex. I'm not compatible with you in that way."

"Oh." Sadness and concern soften her expression. "I'm... I'm so sorry to hear that."

"I'm the one who's sorry, Acushla. I would give my life to be able to please you."

"But you *do* please me." She rises from the sofa and curls onto my lap.

As she wraps her hands around my neck, and rests her head against my chest, I shift to make sure the monster can't press into her flesh.

"Don't be sorry, Rock," she whispers against my ear. "Everything about you pleases me. You please me very much."

CHAPTER TWENTY-TWO

Selina

"Can I borrow your phone?" I shout as I limp. Hunger floods my body as the man I called out to stops at the end of the alley and considers my request.

With a muscular build under a loose-fitting T-shirt and worn jeans, the man looks like maybe he's come out of a sports bar, but he's not super drunk. Just inebriated enough to step into a dark alley to help a stranger. I hope. And most importantly, he's alone.

He steps a few feet into the alley. "Sure." He pulls out his phone. "Come here."

To make my injury seem worse, I stumble on my next step and catch myself against the dumpster. "Could you come to me? I twisted my ankle pretty bad. My boyfriend lives a few blocks away. He'll come as soon as I call him."

I bank on my instincts. This man seems kind, not a predator. Not at all the type of meal container I used to go for. But I won't feel bad about taking his vein. I know now that it's as harmless as donating blood—in fact he *will* be donating blood. Donating his blood to me.

He shines the flashlight on his phone around, checking to confirm I'm alone, then he slowly walks toward me.

I'm not alone—not at all—but my companions are well hidden and won't pose any danger to my meal container, not unless he tries to hurt me. I take comfort in their presence, even though I can handle myself with this man.

Rock's positioned at the other end of the alley. If needed he could be on this man in seconds. Gray's on the rooftop above me and could be down even faster, and both Astrid and Malcolm are opposite the alley across the street. They were the ones who signaled to me that the man was approaching and alone.

But I can't shake the feeling that there's someone else around. Someone watching—following us, following me.

Pike. But it's probably just paranoia. With my new friends, my love and my lover nearby, I know that I'm safe. If Pike came after me when I escaped, he gave up.

The man reaches me, stopping a few feet away, and I lean back against the dumpster, favoring the supposedly injured leg.

"What happened?" he asks.

"So dumb." I dangle a pair of sky-high heels from my hand. "I'm too much of a klutz for this kind of shoe."

"Those look painful." His smile is warm, adding to my gut belief that he's a nice guy and would feed me willingly if he understood how vampires and humans are meant to coexist.

"Believe me, they are." I pretend to put weight on my allegedly hurt ankle and wince.

He holds out the phone toward me.

In a flash, I lift the man by his shoulders and position

him in the shadowed corner next to the dumpster. Here, we're out of sight of the security camera mounted at the back of a trendy furniture store, and shaded from the streetlights at the corner.

Before he can react, I plunge my fangs into his neck and drink.

The warm liquid immediately fulfills my hunger, giving me what I need. Malcolm and Astrid have stopped suggesting that I go to FJS to feed on their staff, and everyone now seems to agree that the more I stay hidden from the vampire community, the better. At least until Xavier's in custody or dead.

Satiated, I lick the man's wounds to heal them and then gently rest him against the wall. He'll wake in about fifteen minutes with no memory of the bite, and probably no memory of why he came into the alley. Malcolm and Astrid will wait to make sure no one mugs him.

I step back into the light.

Rock's at my side in an instant. "Get what you needed?"

I nod. I've been meaning to ask Gray whether or not I can get my nourishment from Rock, mitigating the risk we all take going out to the streets for my meals, but if Rock's species isn't compatible with mine for sex, perhaps his blood isn't either. And more importantly, Rock hasn't offered to feed me.

He said sex is repulsive to him. Then, to clarify he said our species aren't compatible, so it's probably more that sex with a *vampire's* repulsive, so I suspect feeding one would be, too.

And even if I'm wrong about that, I don't want to give up these outings in the fresh night air. As much as I love living with Rock, after fourteen months in actual captivity, my life with Rock seems so small, so contained two stories underground.

I wonder how far I'd have to run to make sure Xavier and Pike never find me.

Gray drops from the rooftop to land two feet in front of us. Rock instinctively pulls me back.

"Holy shit, man," he says to Gray. "Don't startle me like that."

"Sorry." The vampire grins, but his expression and the flash in his deep blue eyes make it clear he's not sorry at all. He scared Rock on purpose, and I love this boyish side of Gray. His sense of play.

He falls into step on the other side of me. "All powered up and ready to train, princess?"

"Guess so." I look up at his sharp, handsome features. I feel a tug in my bloodstream—and another between my legs. It's been a week since we made love, almost two since I fed from his vein, and I want both so badly it's sometimes hard to concentrate on anything else.

I take Rock's hand.

Our shadows stretch ahead of us and the image of the three of us together makes me so happy. On one side I've got a massive wall of a man, close to two feet taller than me, and on the other a well-built but comparatively slim man who'd be considered tall, if it weren't for Rock. Gray must be six foot three or four.

My body casts a diminutive shadow between theirs. Diminutive but strong. And growing stronger every day.

We reach the warehouse where we've been training the past week, ever since the night the cops showed up in the bar, and Gray checks around us before using a combination to open the door.

Gray holds it open for me, then pushes in front of Rock to follow directly behind me.

"Asshole," Rock says, but his tone makes it clear he doesn't mean it.

"Snooze you lose," Gray says as he wraps his arms around my body from behind. "Princess, you smell so good when you're freshly fed." His nose dips below my hair and he licks the skin over my pulsing vein.

"None of that," Malcolm says from the door. I didn't realize he'd followed us over here.

"You're no fun," Gray says to him as he lets me go.

Gray backs away, his eyes focused on me and his tongue dragging slowly over his released fangs.

"Hey, Malc," Rock says. "You here to train with us?"

"Not exactly. Astrid and I need to talk to you about something. As soon as she gets here."

Gray jumps up to grab a rafter more than forty feet above the floor.

"Show-off," Rock mutters.

"Come on, princess." Gray moves, hand over hand, along the rafter like it's monkey bars in a park. "Dare you to join me."

I look up. He's more than two stories off the ground. I haven't attempted anything like that. Not yet. And while I've jumped down one story with ease, I feel sure I'll end up with a sprained ankle, or worse, if I land from that height—assuming I can get up there in the first place.

I meet Gray's daring gaze, and he licks his fangs again as he stares into my eyes with so much desire my body feels like it would do anything to get up to him.

What the hell. At worst, an injury will kill the first half hour or so of tonight's training session.

I bend my legs and leap, reaching up for the rafter. But I

miss it and my hands strike the metal ceiling ten feet *above* that. Stunned, I almost miss it again as I drop, but manage to grab it with one hand.

Gray's there in a split second, hanging from one arm, his other wrapped around my waist.

I kiss him, adrenaline coursing through me like hot spice.

As we each hold on to the rafter with one hand, I wrap my legs around him and deepen our kiss, more turned on than ever, and forgetting I'm forty feet off the ground—and being watched from below.

He breaks the kiss and looks at me with hunger in his eyes. "Good job, princess. I knew you could do it."

I look down, then grab the rafter with both hands, my fingers gripping tightly. Rock and Malcolm seem so far away and fear creeps back inside me. "How do we get down?"

"Drop. You'll be fine as long as you stay relaxed when you land."

"If you say so."

"I *do* say so. But just in case you die, one last kiss." Pulling me against him, he kisses me hard, pushing his tongue into my mouth and gripping my ass with his free hand.

Rubbing his fingers between my legs from behind, he grinds against me, and I raise one leg to wrap around him and give his hardness better access.

I gasp in pleasure as we slide our bodies together. I want to push off my leggings and pull down his pants. My libido revved up from my feeding, I want him inside me, now.

He moves his lips to my ear. "This is giving me some great ideas," he growls.

"Me too." The danger is heightening my desire.

"Some day, princess." He licks my ear, then my throat. "Some day I'll fuck you up in the rafters. That is a promise."

I laugh. "A promise or a threat?" I remember how Pike delivered a similar threat and I shudder.

"Potato, potawto." He winks, then drops, landing in a wide-legged crouch more than two stories beneath me.

"Careful." Rock shouts up. "Aim for me, and I'll catch you."

"I've got a better idea." Gray leaps. In an instant he's hanging in front of me, again. "See if you can take Rock down," he whispers.

"What?"

"One advantage of height is the element of surprise. Attacking an opponent from above."

"But Rock knows I'm up here. Where's the surprise in that?"

"I'll distract him." With a grin, Gray drops again. Then in a flash he moves away from his landing place. I twist around, trying to spot where he went.

The lights go off.

"Hey!" Rock shouts. He's looking up, searching for me in the rafters, but in contrast to mine, it will take his eyes several seconds to adjust to the low light.

Take Rock down? Even with gravity and surprise on my side, it's hard to imagine how I could tackle my giant, but I'm losing my window of opportunity.

Aiming behind him, I drop, landing silently in a crouch. Then I shift my weight to my hands behind me as I scissor my legs around his calves and pull his feet out from under him.

Rock thuds to the concrete floor like a fallen redwood

tree, and I pounce on top of him, pinning one of his arms behind his broad back.

"Bravo!" Gray shouts.

"Are you okay?" I ask as Rock's prone body heaves under mine.

"I'm fine." His voice is tight. He tries to flip over, to pull his arm from my hold, but to my surprise, he can't. I'm too strong.

"I've got you now," I whisper in his ear.

"You already had me," he growls. "Forever."

I let his arm slip out of my hold, and he turns to his back beneath me. I bend to kiss him and he wraps his arms around me.

He flips me onto my back and pins me, one leg across my pelvis and his hands holding my shoulders. "Never let your guard down." He grins.

I lift my legs and kick up to stand, throwing his massive weight off my body and settling on my feet as he lands on his ass.

A proud grin rises from inside me. My strength is beyond what I thought possible.

The lights come back on, and I reach down to help Rock to his feet. He pulls me forward, and I let it happen, going off balance and landing on top of his body.

"You didn't even try," he says.

"Or maybe I ended up exactly where I wanted to be." Grinning, I bend down for another kiss.

He rolls me onto my back and kisses me, making sure he keeps his body weight off me, although I suspect I could take all three hundred and fifty pounds of him without being crushed. At least, that's my guess at Rock's all-muscle weight.

As our kiss deepens, I feel a hardening between his legs,

and I slide against it, loving the low groan that rumbles from inside him. But he rolls to his back and pushes me off him.

I use the momentum to fly back, twisting in the air in a tight spiral to land in a combat-ready crouch. Rock slow-claps as he rises to his feet. Then he tugs at his pants to better hide the bulge. He must be wearing some kind of jockstrap because the bulge is more like a melon than a rod.

While I've still got my eyes on Rock's crotch, Gray grabs me from behind, pinning my arms and locking his lips on my throat. I bend and twist, trying to gain the upper hand, but Gray's still stronger, so I use my ultimate weapon against him.

I slide one arm behind me and rub his package, loving how it hardens instantly, even constrained in a jockstrap.

"None of that, princess." He slides one of his hands to my breast—hypocrite—and then reaches his mouth around to capture mine from the side.

His body grinds against my groping hand as his tongue and lips plunder. If my arms were free I'd be pulling off our clothing.

"You call this training?" Astrid asks.

I break the kiss. "When did you get here?"

"I've been here long enough to know you three need a better chaperone." She shakes her head at Malcolm, who shrugs.

"Yeah," Malcolm says. "If you can get your minds out of your dicks for a minute, Astrid has something important to tell you."

"I don't have a dick," I say to Malcolm as Gray slowly releases me, tweaking my nipple before he lets me go.

"What's up?" Rock asks Astrid.

Astrid gestures for us to follow and we all sit on wooden

folding chairs at the side of the room. Everyone except Rock, that is, who sits on the floor. He'd crush these chairs.

"We've been hearing troubling things at FJS."

Gray leans toward me. "Astrid's head of security there."

I nod.

"What kind of things?" Rock asks.

"Some of my staff have heard whispers—about Selina."

I suck in a sharp breath. "Why would anyone at FJS be talking about me?"

Astrid shakes her head. "That's what I'm worried about. Certainly none of us have mentioned you." She glances at Malcolm and Gray, who both nod.

"Then what's going on?" Gray leans forward in his chair, the first time I've seen him sit in anything but a totally relaxed position.

"FJS security has informants on the street," Astrid says.

"Informants?" I ask.

She nods. "Lone vampires. Plus a few who give us information about their syndicates."

"Spies?" I ask.

She shrugs. "Confidential informants. And one told us he's been asked to stay on the lookout for a young female vampire." Astrid pauses. "One with purple hair."

I gasp, and Rock takes my hand. "Who?" he booms. "Who's asking about Selina? And who is this informant working for? Where do I find him?"

"Cool your jets, Rock," Astrid responds. "I'm looking into it, but I've got to assume it's Xavier who's asking around. Who else would it be?" She looks at Gray.

Rock rubs my hand with his thumb. "I'll keep her safe. From now on, Selina doesn't leave my apartment."

"Rock." I bite my tongue. I don't want to complain, but the idea of never leaving his apartment? It's been hard enough to only leave under supervision, and only to feed or come to these training sessions. If I can't leave the apartment, I'm still Xavier's prisoner, even if I'm with Rock.

"And that's not all," Malcolm adds.

"Holy hell," Grayson says. "What the fuck else?"

Malcolm straightens. "That rogue vamp killed again, about a week ago. We just heard. This time it doesn't even look like they fed, just tore out the human's throat and left the body to bleed."

Everyone shivers, shocked at the brutality.

"What's that got to do with Selina?" Rock asks.

"Nothing. Not directly. But the cops have upped their vampire hunting patrols. Until this killer's caught, none of us are safe."

"The latest victim was another young woman," Astrid says. "Her body was found in a park."

I shudder.

"What is it?" Rock asks, kneeling to wrap his arm around me.

"It's just all so..." I shake my head, not willing to tell even Rock what I'm thinking.

My dream. In my dream I drank from a young woman on a park bench. It's a coincidence but still creepy.

"Don't worry, princess. If the cops don't catch this vamp, Astrid's team will. After that, the cops will dial their vampire killing rate back down to normal." Gray lays his hand on my shoulder. "And as for Xavier and Pike, Rock and I will keep you safe."

His words are comforting, but I know he's making a promise he has no way to keep.

CHAPTER TWENTY-THREE

Colton

O'Malley's, the bar across the street from me, is quiet. Not one human, never mind vampire, has come or gone from the bar in the twenty minutes I've been watching. The Vampire Task Force got a tip from an anonymous female caller that this place serves vamps. Disgusting.

I can't imagine anything more despicable than humans associating with those hideous creatures. This city won't be safe until every last vamp is staked, and one of them will be the bloodsucker that killed my sister.

My partner, Sanjay, and I checked out this bar when the tip first came in. That night, we handed out cards, questioned the staff and customers. We got nothing, but since I'm off duty and the bar's on my way home, I figured I'd give it another shot. No stone unturned.

Crossing the street, I check the stakes stashed in the lining of my leather jacket. Like any police constable, I can't carry my firearm when I'm off duty, but sharp wooden stakes are another matter. No messy paperwork or internal affairs investigations when a cop stakes a bloodsucker. Just a commendation from the mayor.

Inside the bar, a rhythmic song, maybe old-school Motown, thumps through the air, loud enough to add atmosphere but not a total conversation killer. The place isn't fancy, it's got a friendly vibe, and it's hard to imagine that the owner of a place like this would knowingly serve bloodsucking monsters.

Quickly scanning, I note nine patrons. A group of five men in matching red and white baseball uniforms debate the Raptors' chances this season. An older couple, the male Asian, female Caucasian, sit in a booth, both looking down at their phones instead of each other. Two women in their mid forties, both with fake blond hair and dressed like they're still twenty, perch atop bar stools, engaging the bartender—a tall, First Nations man who's half-heartedly grinning at the flirting women. He looks up at me and nods.

Nothing suspicious.

The waitress, a curvaceous Caucasian woman, steps in from the hallway at the back. Her black T-shirt, worn a few inches above jeans, has a faded rock band logo. She gives off a biker chick vibe, but crossed with something else—mafia wife? I grin inwardly.

Looking down as she walks, she adjusts whatever is gathering her unnaturally black hair onto the top of her head and nearly crashes into me.

"Hey. Sorry." She smiles. "You." She tips her head to the side. "You've been in here before, right?"

I nod.

"Came back to see me, I hope?" Her eyebrows rise subtly to deliver the not-so-subtle message that she's flirting. Either because she's interested or because she's hoping to get a better tip. In spite of my police training, I'm not good at telling the difference.

"You caught me."

"Sit anywhere you like," she says. "What can I get you?" I've forgotten her name and she's older than I remembered. Or maybe her over-tanned complexion directly under a light just makes her seem older.

I step toward the bar and lean against it as she walks in behind. "Got a half-decent craft ale on tap?"

"Hoppy or malty?"

"Malty."

She smiles. "I've got just the thing. Kev, a pint of Caramel Craze for my friend here."

The bartender nods and leaves his admirers for a moment to grab a chilled glass and pull the beer.

I take a seat at a table close to the back hallway where I can take in the entire room. This really isn't the kind of place that vampires frequent. It couldn't be a more normal-looking neighborhood waterhole if it tried.

"Let me know what you think." The waitress sets down my beer. "I'll get you something else if you don't like it." Her fingers, tipped with chipped navy nail polish, rest on my table as she waits for me to taste the beer.

"It's good. Thanks." If nothing else, this visit will yield a good drink. The waitress starts to leave.

"Hey."

She turns back.

"Got a minute?" I gesture toward the empty chair at my table.

Smiling, she pulls out the chair and sits.

"What can I do you for?" She leans forward. "You looking for company?"

"Served any vampires tonight?"

She blinks—hard. A clear reaction, but I can't be positive what it means. Not yet. My question was blunt, but her reaction switched my cop instincts on to high. Is she the one who called in the anonymous tip? Or is *she* the one who serves vamps?

"Vampires?" Her voice is tight. "Ha! None tonight. Why? You into that kind of thing? Kinky."

I smile, hoping to keep her talking. "I'm serious. There's been an increase in vampire attacks in the city."

"Really?" She shivers. "Shit... Sounds like I'd better keep my eyes open."

I nod. "We suspect the attacks could be the work of one vampire, but it's hard to know when you're dealing with monsters."

She leans back. "That's horrifying."

"Sure is." I narrow my eyes. "And when I find the creature, I'll stake him myself."

"How brave." She's teasing me.

Cupping my pint of beer, I lean forward. "You sure you haven't seen anything? Any customers who only come in after dark?"

"We've got lots of those. It's a bar."

I take another sip of the beer. "Any customers who act suspicious?"

She shakes her head, but her posture's tense. She's holding something back. But what?

"Have you ever met a vampire?" she asks.

Frowning, I shake my head. "No, you?"

"How would I know? I mean—how would I know *for sure*?" She's acting frightened at the idea, emphasis on acting. She's not really frightened, but I can't figure out if she's joking or hiding something.

"Do vampires wear capes?" she asks, wide-eyed. "Do

they have long, fanged overbites? Widow's peaks?" Clearly she thinks this is funny.

"Vampires aren't always obvious." I tamp down my irritation. "Bloodsuckers can hide amongst us. That's what makes them the single biggest threat to humanity."

She leans back in her chair. "Even for a cop, you sure seem to hate vampires a lot."

"One killed my kid sister."

Her expression completely shifts. "Oh, I'm so sorry. When? How did it happen?"

My throat tightens. "Four years ago. She was only nineteen."

"That's terrible. Did they catch the vampire who did it?"

I shake my head. Every time a bloodsucker gets staked I hope we've taken out the right one, but the monster who killed a woman in the park last week is the same one who killed Shelly. I'm sure of it.

"Do vampires kill often?" she asks me.

"More often than people think."

The front door to the bar opens and a group of three enters. The first is a huge man, Caucasian, with blond hair and a serious five-o'clock shadow. If memory serves, he's the owner. The next, also a Caucasian male, is well dressed with dark, side-swept hair, sideburns and...I suck in a breath...the third person who enters is the most beautiful girl I have ever seen.

It's more than her beauty I'm drawn to—although that is spectacular—it's more like she radiates goodness. I want to talk to her more than I've ever wanted anything, and the pull nearly lifts me off my chair. But the two men she came in with flank her protectively as they walk toward the booth at the back, not far from my table.

When they sit, the waitress notices them and jumps to

her feet. "Hey boss," she says. She tries to send the big man a message with her eyes, but I can't figure out what she's trying to say.

"Hey, Chelle," the owner responds. "Quiet night?"

"Pretty quiet," she answers. "Whiskeys all round?"

"Champagne for me, luv." The elegant, dark-haired man has a British accent.

"Champagne?" The waitress laughs. "Sorry, dude. White wine spritzer is as close as we get to that in here."

"Ask Kev to open a bottle of the Okanagan chardonnay," the big man says, then turns to the other guy. "I think you'll like it."

This banter about drinks plays in the background as my attention stays tuned to the woman. The rest of the bar has gone into soft focus while she remains crystal clear. Her light purple hair suits her so well I can almost believe she was born with it, and her pale skin seems to glow. Icy blue eyes flash with intelligence and humor, and although her physique is slight, making her seem vulnerable, her posture hints at confidence and strength.

I'm in love.

Laughing at myself, I shake my head. I don't believe in love at first sight, and even if it might exist for some people, it won't ever for me. I'm not that kind of guy. I've never been in love, never mind at first sight. Plus, I don't have time for dating. Not while there are vampires on the loose.

But still, I can't help staring, wondering if one of the two men is her boyfriend. They're both paying her plenty of attention. Too much attention if you ask me. The British one has pressed his leg against hers under the table and the big man looks like he'll kill anyone who comes near her.

The waitress, Chelle, sets two glasses of whiskeys down for them—they look like triples—and a glass of wine. The beautiful girl must be a regular if the waitress knows her order. Maybe I should become a regular, too.

Chelle drops the tray to her side as she turns away from the table, and her eyes narrow. She looks pissed. At what?

I signal her with my fingers.

She nods and her expression changes. “Another beer?”

“That would be great. Thanks.” I hadn’t planned on having a second, but as non-vampy as this place seems, I still think Chelle could be hiding something, and if I’m honest with myself, the purple-haired girl’s arrival made the place a hundred times more interesting.

“Hey, Chelle?” I touch the waitress’s arm to stop her from heading straight to the bar after she brings my beer.

“You remembered my name?” Her ample chest expands as she smiles. She cocks one hip and tips her head to the side.

Shit. Now she thinks *I’m* flirting. There’s no point in correcting her.

She leans onto the table, pushing her chest forward and arching her back. “Anything else I can do for you? Anything at all?”

Her meaning is clear, and I grin, hoping to use this rapport to get her to open up. It’s not the first time I’ve used my looks to get better cooperation from a witness or informant. It never seems right, using people like that, and feels even more gross than normal tonight, because the purple-haired girl could be watching us, and for some reason I care what she thinks about me.

“Thanks for listening earlier,” I say softly. “About my sister.”

“Sure, honey.” Her hand slides on top of mine. “You can talk to me anytime. I’m a real good listener. Good at other stuff, too.” She licks her lips and her eyes fill with lust.

I take my hand from under hers and pull out my card. "If you hear or see anything suspicious, even if you just have a hunch...call me. Anytime. Okay?"

"*Anytime*?" Chelle eyes me hungrily as she takes my card, and her teeth scrape her lower lip. She's *definitely* got the wrong idea about why I gave her my card, and I'm starting to think she's not capable of hiding anything, never mind vampires.

But one way or another, I'm going to come back to this bar.

Vampire rumors aside, I need a chance to talk to that purple-haired woman, preferably when those men aren't boxing her in. And if there's even a small chance that vampires do come in here, I need to protect her.

CHAPTER TWENTY-FOUR

Selina

"That guy's staring at you." Rock gestures with his head toward the table not ten feet away from us. "Ever since we came in."

"No, he's not." I glance over, and the man immediately looks down to take a sip of his beer. "Maybe he's been looking at Gray." I nudge the vampire's knee under the table. "Gray's pretty hot."

"Why thank you, princess." Gray slides his hand along my upper thigh and my body involuntarily leans against his.

The man watching me from the next table is incredibly good-looking.

I'm seated with two men who both make my body sing, yet I can't help noticing this stranger's short blond hair that hints at curls on top, and his square-jawed face and clear skin that make him seem boyish, even though his physique is all man.

When I first came in, he smiled at me, and his broad and dimpled expression was such a genuine exhibition of joy I wondered for an instant if he knew me. But I've never met anyone with his clean-cut handsomeness before. I'd remember.

"Do you think..." I glance over at him again and our eyes meet for a moment. "Could he be working for King Xavier?"

"I keep telling you," Gray nudges me. "That asshole's not a king."

"Regardless. Do you think Xavier and Pike might have humans working for them? Looking for me?"

Rock shakes his head. "No. The guy's a cop. He's the one who gave me his card last week. Colton something."

A cop. My belly tightening, I suck in a sharp breath. Can this Colton guy tell what Gray and I are? Is he just waiting for the chance to stake us?

"Why do you think he came back here?" I ask Rock.

"Probably invited by Chelle," Gray says. "She looks like she's ready to eat him."

I glance toward the bar and realize that Gray is right. Chelle is staring at the cop with obvious interest. Then again, it's hard to imagine any straight woman not wanting to look at this objectively good-looking man—as much and as often as possible.

Even Kev's barfly groupies are glancing over their shoulders at the man, whispering conspiratorially to each other. Kev doesn't seem to mind that he's temporarily lost the attention of his fan club.

The cop gestures for Chelle, and she rushes to his table, an inviting smile on her lips. When he asks for his bill, Chelle looks disappointed.

"Thanks," she says after accepting what looks like a generous tip.

"And give me a call if—"

"Definitely." She leans toward him. "In fact, I get off in an hour. If you stick around—"

"Sorry," he says through a smile that now seems forced, uncomfortable. "Got work tomorrow. Past my bedtime."

"Bedtime sounds good to me." Chelle raises her eyebrows.

His cheeks flush, making him seem even more boyish, and it's beyond adorable. This man looks like he just walked off a film set where he's playing the guy with the heart of gold, the one who gets the girl and then wins the big game.

I hope he doesn't get together with Chelle. She'd eat him alive.

"Have to go." He stands, and I take in the full expanse of Colton.

Broad shouldered and chested, his torso tapers down to his solid waist and hips, then his thighs press out hard against denim. His body screams football player, or some kind of athlete, and it's easy to imagine the muscles under his T-shirt and jeans, even though he's wearing a leather jacket over top.

As he walks toward the exit, the back of him is even more impressive. Solid mounds of glutes curve above well-defined hamstrings that flex as he walks, and those lead down to well-shaped calves.

"Earth to Selina." Gray draws my attention.

I smile, embarrassed that he caught me gawking. Possibly drooling. "Sorry. I'm just worried that there was a cop in here."

"I'll ask Chelle what he wanted." Rock stands and crosses to the bar.

"You okay, princess?" Gray strokes my thigh

My sex contracts and I realize I'm wet. But I can't tell whether it's because my lover's hand is on my thigh or because I was imagining the cop's naked body. Probably both.

Gray presses his lips close to my ear. "Fancy a quickie?" His long finger flicks high on my thigh and my insides contract again.

Rock strides back toward us and the bench groans as he slides into the booth. "Cop is off duty. Claims he lives around here. Chelle says he hates vampires even more then most cops, if that's possible. She didn't tell him anything."

"How do we know that?" My chest tightens. "Chelle hates me."

Rock tips his head to the side. "What makes you say that?"

"Chelle likes you, Rock. I mean, really *likes* you. She hates that we're together."

Frowning, he glances back at his waitress, then turns to me. "I trust Chelle. You don't have to worry."

"Easy for you to say, big man." Gray's finger slides close to my sex. "You're not the one he wants to stake."

"Only because he thinks I'm human." Rock looks down at the table to hide the pain in his eyes.

"Come on, Rock," Gray says. "It's not the same for you. We all know that cop is licensed to stake either Selina or me on sight."

Rock shrugs, but I sense his pain. Alone all my life, never belonging anywhere, even I can't imagine what it's like to not even know *what* you are. At least I knew I was human and now a vampire. Even if I was totally alone for so long in both worlds, Rock carries a deep mantle of sadness and shame I don't fully understand. But I hope beyond hope I can help him lift it.

I turn to Gray. "See you at training tomorrow?"

"Is that a hint for me to leave, princess?"

I fake a yawn. "I am tired."

"So, I take it that's a *no* to my earlier suggestion." His fingers caress high on my thigh.

"Not a *no*, just a *not tonight*."

"Your loss." He bends close. "My cock's loss, too." He slips out of the booth and stands at the edge of the table. "I'll see you two tomorrow at dusk. Unless Selina's new crush is outside waiting to stake me."

My cheeks flare with heat. "My new what?"

He laughs, then bends to cup my chin. "It's okay pet. I get it. I'd fuck that cop too. He's hot." Gray strides out of the bar with infuriating confidence as I regain my composure after his accusation. I got defensive because he was right.

I clear my throat and turn to Rock. "Should we make sure Gray's okay? What if Colton *is* waiting outside?"

Rock shakes his head. "Gray can handle himself—unless the cop set up an ambush involving a hundred of this friends and a dozen silver nets."

"That image isn't exactly comforting." I look toward the door, wishing I could see through it, wishing I had a way to know Gray was safe.

"If the cop set a trap, then Gray's already dead," Rock says without emotion.

I suck in a breath.

He stretches across the table and takes my hands. "Acushla. He's fine. With Gray's training and experience, he would have sensed a group of humans lurking outside."

I nibble my lower lip. "I know. It's just...today's been a lot."

"Let's go downstairs." He slides out of the booth and I follow.

Rock envelops me in his arms, and I feel safe in his embrace, his huge, warm body shielding mine from the rest of the world. But no matter how good it feels, I can't live my entire life in Rock's arms.

"You okay to close up?" he calls over to Kev.

"Sure, boss. No problem."

We head down to the apartment, and he takes out the bedding for me to use on the sofa.

As he bends to set it down, I lay my hand on his back. "Can I sleep with you tonight?"

His ribs expand as he inhales, then he turns and sets his hands on my shoulders. "Acushla, we've talked about this."

"I'm not talking about sex. I just want to hold you. I want you to hold me. I want to fall asleep in your arms where I know I'm safe."

The word *safe* has an obvious impact, and I see in his eyes the possibility that he might yield. I press my head against his chest, loving how his two hearts thump at different rates, especially when he's aroused.

I love that he's turned on, even if he won't act on it. I've accepted that for now. It's sad, but I'm not going to push Rock into doing something that makes him uncomfortable.

Without a word, he slips his arm over my shoulders and leads me toward his bedroom. Without speaking, we undress, but he leaves his boxers on, then we both slide under his cozy duvet with its crisp white cover. He turns out his bedside lamp, a beautiful object I'm pretty sure is an original Frank Lloyd Wright.

I shift toward him, and he doesn't object as I snuggle into his side, using his chest for a pillow.

"Thank you," I say softly.

He responds by gliding his hand over my back, and I squeeze my legs together to contain the pleasure.

I trace my finger along a scar on Rock's chest. "How did this happen?"

"I'm not even sure anymore." His voice tightens. Clearly he's not in the mood to open up, and if I push too hard, I might find myself kicked out of his bed.

"Do you think it's Pike who's been asking around about me?"

"Who else could it be?" His voice is low—soft but deliciously deep.

"No one, I guess. Silly for me to think there could be anyone else. It's not like I'm anyone special." I slide one of my legs over his, loving the tickle of the hairs over his hard muscles, and am grateful when he doesn't push my leg back off.

"But you *are* special." He kisses the top of my head. "Very special."

"You know what I mean. And besides, you have to say that. You *love* me."

"Yes, I do. Very much." His fingers stroke my spine again, and his gentle caress contrasts against the heat and power radiating from his body and the rumble of his deep voice. I've never been more in love. Or more turned on.

I'm not sure I'll be able to sleep in this state, but I don't want to do anything that might ruin this intimacy between us. I feel like I belong here in his bed, in his arms.

Tipping my head up, I kiss him softly. I've never felt quite so safe or so warm. Some day I do hope we can consummate our love. He claims we aren't compatible, but I sense that the real reason behind his sex avoidance is more complicated than that.

As much as I yearn for Rock, as much as I lust at the thought of his massive body moving above me, inside me, I love him enough to give him space, to let the sex between us happen on his terms, when he's ready. We have nothing but time. And with him I am safe.

CHAPTER TWENTY-FIVE

Rock

"That cop came by the bar again."

"So?" Grayson leans against a pillar in the warehouse as Selina takes a well-deserved break from training. Then again, she just took an entire night off.

"You don't find it troubling that a cop from the Vampire Task Force is hanging around my bar? Right above where Selina lives?"

"You've got a point." Grayson folds his arms over his chest. "Selina should move in with me."

"Very funny." But his idea isn't totally crazy. We can't go on this way forever. I know Selina loves me, but I also know she feels trapped living her days in my basement and her nights in my bar.

Last night, when she needed to feed, Gray took her to a human nightclub, and as much as I hated the idea of letting her out of my sight, Gray kept her safe. I don't really want to think too hard about what I'm certain they did after she fed, but remain glad that Gray can satisfy my love's needs in ways that I can't.

And I'm sure Gray could house her somewhere she'd be more free to move around, to see other people, to have a life outside mine.

I want that for her. I wish I could give those things to her, but Gray can.

"I don't think she should move into FJS corporate housing," I tell Gray.

His expression twists in disgust. "You think I live in corporate housing?" He straightens off the pillar and tugs on the cuffs of his casual shirt, as if popping his cuffs. "I've got a house, a mansion really. In Rosedale. Big enough that you could live there too, if you want."

"What? The three of us shacking up together?"

He shrugs. "Is it the worst idea you've ever heard?"

As he asks the question, I realize it isn't. "How many bedrooms?"

"Six."

"And you live there alone?"

"At the moment, yes. All the windows are treated. No risk of sunlight burns, and it's not a dungeon."

"Hey."

Gray raises his hands. "I'm just calling it like I see it, mate. You're the one who chose to live two stories underground, and you're not even harmed by sunlight. Just saying."

I look over to my love. She's back at work, practicing a running, twisting kick that Gray taught her. She hits her target every time.

Selina was strong when I met her, compared to a human anyway, but I can't deny how her power changed after she drank from Grayson, and how her abilities have improved since we started this training and she's been feeding from humans more regularly.

If we all lived together, would she drink from Gray's vein all the time? Would he drink from hers? Would she sleep in his bed instead of mine? We've shared a bed for over a week now. She's respected my boundaries, and holding her as she sleeps, waking up with her in my arms, has been amazing.

Gray and Selina are already having sex every chance they get. If living together strengthens their emotional bonds, will I lose her?

She leaps into the air, spins at least five times, then thrusts out her leg, striking the practice dummy in the head. She's amazing.

And I'm being a selfish child.

I can't put my happiness over hers. It's not like I could ever fulfill all Selina's needs or be a true mate for her, anyway. After we finish training, I'll ask her whether she likes the idea of us moving in with Gray.

The sound of splintering glass fills the air.

Shards rain down onto the concrete floor as several vampires fly through the broken windows and land on the floor, all fully armed with wooden stakes and crossbows.

Ignoring me, the vamps head for Selina. I race forward. I grab two of them and smash their heads together. Gray arrives like a flash, quickly staking one, then chasing after another.

Where is Selina?

Using one of the moves Gray taught her, Selina takes out a tall vamp with a side sweep aimed low on his legs to steal his balance. Leaping over him in a cartwheel motion, she grabs the stake from his hand, but before she can stab him two other vampires are aiming loaded crossbows at her chest.

Another one grabs her from behind and holds his stake ready to drive through her back and into her heart.

"Grayson!" I shout. "Selina's trapped!"

The vamp Gray's chasing lunges at me. I throw him back with a swipe of my arm. The vamp smashes into one of the metal pillars. Gray stakes him, then pulls the weapon from the dead vamp's chest.

Gray leaps toward Selina. But she's got at least three stakes aimed straight at her heart. Gray stops short.

My hearts pound as I look for a solution. There are two vampires barely four feet in front of her with crossbows, and another's got his arm across her neck and a wooden stake pressed into her from behind

"Back off," the one holding Selina yells, and I'm surprised to hear it's a female voice. "Back off or she's dead."

"You're not going to kill her," Grayson says. "Xavier wants her alive."

"Want to make a bet?" One of the vampires holding a crossbow sharpens his aim, finger on the trigger. The point 's not four feet from Selina's heart. "One false move and she's dead."

"Come on," Grayson walks slowly toward them. "Let's talk. No need for anymore of you to die. You can have her—for a reasonable price. Let's talk numbers."

Selina's eyes turn toward Gray, and anger swells inside me. I know Gray doesn't mean that—at least I hope he doesn't—but I wish I understood his plan. My only tactic against a vampire is using my size and strength, and that only works when I catch one by surprise, negating their far superior speed and agility.

I feel so useless. It's too risky for me to tackle any of the vamps around her at the moment. I'm not fast enough, and if one of those crossbows is fired...

Gray leaps, landing between the stake-wielding attackers and Selina. He grabs for one of the crossbows.

The vampire tries to duck around Gray, and his weapon shoots, the stake flying through the warehouse, narrowly missing me before striking the wall.

Something else smashes through the darkened windows above, and the lights in the warehouse space go out.

Now the room's barely illuminated through the broken windows, and fear invades my chest as I realize I'm now at even more of a disadvantage as the only one in the room who can't see in the dark.

Hearing a yell, I turn toward the sound as my eyes adjust. A beam of moonlight illuminates the center of the room. One of the crossbow-wielding vampires is trapped under a net that looks like it's made of silver. The metal must be coated in acid because it's burning through the vamp's leather garb, and then the silver's burning into his skin. Smoke rises as he screams in agony.

Gray disarms and then stakes the other attacker, who was clearly distracted by his buddy's torture under that net.

Those two vamps are neutralized, but Selina's still held from behind, a stake at her heart, and I'm pretty sure there are other vampires alive in the room. I can't see them in the darkness. Or Gray.

From the beam of light, Selina stares right at me. "Pike," she mouths, or at least that's what it looks like to me, and she tips her head up and to the side.

I search around the room, then up high where she gestured, wishing I had night vision.

When I turn back to her, Selina's body twists in pain. That asshole is pushing the stake into her flesh. Her eyes fill with fear, but also a determination to live. I creep forward, but if I come much closer, or make any attempt to get that vamp off her, the stake will be through her heart. I'm fast, but vampires are faster.

Hearing a sound, I spot another vampire near the side of the room. He or she is creeping around, scanning the room, crossbow at the ready, probably looking for the source of that silver net.

Hearing my heavy footsteps approach, the vampire turns and fires in my direction. I duck to the side, but the stake pierces my shoulder.

I barely feel the pain, and without slowing my advance, I tug the wooden weapon out and plunge it into the vampire's heart before he has a chance to reload.

I turn back toward Selina.

She's gone.

While I was fending off that last attack, she got away from the one holding her, but where did she go?

Panicked, I scan the room, searching for her.

Gray is in hand-to-hand combat with two vamps, and I don't think he's yet noticed she's gone.

Hearing a sound near the ceiling, I look up.

Atop one of the rafters, a huge, leather-clad vampire holds Selina under one of his massive arms. Light from outside catches his scarred face.

Is this Pike?

Selina punches and kicks, and the vampire almost loses his balance. He puts a cloth to her mouth and her body goes slack.

The scarred vampire tosses her body over his shoulder, and then leaps through the broken window into the night.

BONUS SCENE:

Would you like to see what happened, when Gray took Selina out to a nightclub last night? (Spoiler alert: it got pretty hot.) And the bonus scene contains more hints about Gray and what he knows about Selina.

I'd love to give you a FREE BONUS scene. https://BookHip.com/DLBQGQS

CAN'T WAIT to see what happens next? Continue Selina's story with Rock and Gray (and Pike and Colton??) in BOUND BY HER PASSION

WITH ROCK AND GRAYSON, I've found men who make my heart flutter and offer the companionship I've always craved. They're so different, and yet I'm falling hard for both. But while the gentle giant Rock can't offer what my body craves, the wealthy and charming Gray is carefully guarding his heart.

Captured by the terrifying Pike, will my growing vampiric power be enough to escape him? Worse, can I resist the inexplicable yearning I feel for my captor?

Meanwhile, the hunky, human Colton keeps paying me attention—and I'm not sure I want him to stop, in spite of his vendetta against vampires. And through it all, King Xavier is hunting me, determined I'll suffer a painful death.

Read now: http://maraleigh.com/bbhb2b

I've also included a special sneak peek of my steamy contemporary romance, BAD BOY NEXT DOOR, at the end of this book.

Sneak Peek

ALSO BY MARA LEIGH

PARANORMAL REVERSE HAREM ROMANCE

Standalone RH Vampire Read

Her Vampire Protectors

Bound by her Blood Series

Bound by Her Blood

Bound by Her Passion

Bound by Her Destiny

Bound by Her Love

Bound by Her Power

The Vampires' Illuminant Series

Auctioned for Her Blood

Trapped for Her Blood

Desired for Her Blood

Devoted to Her Heart

Fighting for Her Heart

Her Psycho Vampire Bodyguards Series

Princess Broken

Princess Claimed

Princess Avenged

CONTEMPORARY ROMANCE

Bad Stepbrother

Downey Brothers Series

Bad Boy Next Door

Bad Habit

Bad Princess (coming soon)

Best Kind of Bad (coming soon)

SHORT EROTIC READS

Fantasies Unleashed Series

Dirty Business

Surrender

Bedded by Strangers

Humbling the Boss

A NOTE TO READERS

Did you enjoy this book?
If so, you can make a huge difference.

Not only do reader reviews make my day, they help bring books to the attention of other readers. In fact, no marketing tool is more powerful or effective than honest reader reviews.

That said, I'd be very grateful if you could spend a one or two minutes leaving a review on this book's Amazon page. (The review can be as short as you like.)

Believe me—your review matters.

And thank you so much for reading!
xo, Mara

Be the first to hear about sales and new releases:
Sign up here
http://maraleigh.com/nlbook

ABOUT THE AUTHOR

Mara Leigh escaped from the corporate world and now hangs out in coffee shops, letting her imagination run wild. After living in various cities including Edinburgh, San Francisco and Philadelphia, Mara and her exorbitant shoe collection have settled in Toronto where she writes sexy, smart and satisfying contemporary and paranormal romance.

Follow her on:
Amazon
BookBub
Newsletter: maraleigh.com/nlbook
Reader Facebook Group:
facebook.com/groups/MaraLeighReaderRoom

Or find her on most social media outlets.
@maraleighauthor

BAD BOY NEXT DOOR

BONUS READ

Nick

An hour before closing, the club was half full, mostly loners with boners.

Stationed inside the front door, I crossed my arms over my chest and my hands barely reached my elbows. Intimidation was at the top of the job description for a strip club bouncer, and my bulked-up bod—a disadvantage for some things—made me an ace at this job. A master.

It'd been a typical night at Solid Gold. I'd wrangled six or seven rowdy bachelor parties, the douches' entitlement raging after paying our sky-high party surcharges. And along with the partiers, there'd been the typical groups of out-of-town businessmen: assholes who arrived acting like they were above it all, then climbed on stage, drooling, after downing a bottle of table-service vodka.

Melodie, a dancer who'd worked here almost as long as I had, arrived at my side, her tits sparkling with sweat and glitter from her last set.

"Hey, Nick." Her eyes were wide and worried, so I bent down to hear her over the pounding music. "Have you seen Angel?"

I shook my head and then scanned the room. Diamond was on stage, gyrating trancelike through her routine, and five other dancers were scattered around, grinding their asses into laps or pressing their tits near the customers' faces. No sign of Angel.

I bent back down. "Why? She missing?"

Melodie bit the side of her hot-pink lip. "She's pretty stoned. Last I saw her, she was doing a champagne-room dance for one of the bachelor parties. Haven't seen her since."

"Shit."

"Yeah. If Stan catches her doing tricks on the side again, she'll be out on her ass."

"I'll check the alley."

I nodded toward the other bouncer, Dom, who took my place at the front door, then I wove through the field of drunken men and writhing women toward the dark hallway that led past the girls' dressing room and the kitchen to the back entrance.

As head of security for Solid Gold, I was supposed to tell our boss, Stan, if the girls broke his rules, but the dancers trusted me not to rat, and that's how I kept them safe from dangers worse than a missed paycheck.

Ninety-five percent of our customers were harmless, horny assholes, but the other five percent were trouble—trouble with a capital dick—men who treated these women like garbage on account of how they made rent.

I pushed open the back door, and it slammed against the metal rail of the fire escape behind it. Sure enough, Angel was staggering on her sky-high heels, attempting a private dance for four men who were laughing and hooting, egging her on.

"Me first," one of them said. "I am so ready to go." He grabbed Angel's arm, yanking her to her knees on the piss-soaked asphalt.

"Party's over, gentlemen." I strode down the alley toward them.

"Fuck off," said the one with his fly open. Bold words given he'd just exposed a handle for me to grab onto.

"Sorry, boys. This isn't going to happen." Reaching under Angel's armpits, I lifted her to her feet. Blood trailed down her shins. Damn. Even if she could take the pain once she came down from this high, Stan wouldn't let her work if her knees scabbed over.

"I'm good," she slurred, her eyes glassy, unfocused. "Don't worry, Nick."

"Four assholes and one barely conscious girl..." Tucking Angel under one arm, I straightened to my full height of six seven and stared at the frat-aged partiers. "Guess I'd better call the cops."

"Buddy, she agreed to do us." The tallest one held up his hands in defense. "Bitch took our money. This is con-sens-u-al." The guy was blond and clean-cut. I'd lay bets his name was Bro.

"Does she look like she's in any shape to be offering consent?" Angel slumped against me, her ankles crying uncle to her platform shoes.

"Whatever," said the asshole with his dick half out. "Then the skank owes us two hundred bucks. Fifty per blow job."

"I paid a hundred to fuck her," said a guy from the shadows. "Either she bends over to take it, or I'm getting my hundred back."

"And I'm calling the cops." I reached for my phone.

"No fucking way." The guy from the shadows ran at me swinging, which was kind of a joke.

Without even releasing my hold on Angel, I raised my other arm to block his punch. The guy swung again, and I grabbed his fist midair and twisted. He dropped to his knees.

"While you're down there"—I nodded toward the asshole zipping his dick into his khakis—"maybe you can suck your friend's cock."

He looked up at me with terror in his eyes.

I kicked him onto his ass. "Get the fuck out of here. Now."

The four men scrambled down the alley, the one who'd tried to punch me limping, and when they got close to the street, the blond bro turned back. "You're going to be sorry, you piece of scum. So will the owner of this piece-of-shit strip club. Our lawyer will be in touch."

Good luck with that, I thought. I'd heard plenty of threats over the years, threats more credible than that one. Men like Bro would never follow through, avoiding shame worth a million times more than whatever damages they thought they were owed.

Angel stroked my chest. "Nick to the rescue."

"What the fuck, Angel?" I helped her walk toward the door on her shaky heels. "Going into the alley with four drunk customers? You got a death wish?"

I immediately wanted to eat my words. Some of these girls actually did have death wishes, at least subconsciously. But I was no shrink. Wasn't my job to fix these girls, just keep them safe. At least that's how I saw my job.

To Stan it was more like: make sure the customers paid

and the girls didn't take any of what he saw as his cash on the side.

"I need the money," Angel mumbled as I helped her up the stairs. "And besides, I took some E. I'm horny." She rubbed up against me. "How 'bout you fuck me, Nick?" She grabbed my package. "My way of saying thanks."

"Cut it out." I pulled her hand off me. "It's the Ecstasy talking."

"No, it's not. Come on." She ground her ass against me. "Let me have a taste of that famous big dick."

I banged on the steel door, and she took the opportunity to grab my hardening cock. After two years, you'd think I'd be immune to the dancers. My brain was, mostly, but my dick couldn't get with the program.

Melodie opened the door a crack. "Thank god, Angel. You okay?"

"Get her bag," I told Melodie, who quickly disappeared into the dressing room.

"At least let me suck you off." Angel slid down my body.

I bent to lift her back up. "Not a chance."

"Why?" she whined. "I know you want it. You're already hard." She kept rubbing me. "Let me take care of you, Nick. Don't you like me? What's wrong with me?"

"You're high."

"So what?" She fondled her barely covered tits, pressing them together. "I'm a better lay when I'm high." She went for my fly, and I grabbed both her wrists in one hand.

Melodie showed up at the door and tossed me Angel's shit. I draped her coat over her shoulders and started to walk her down the alley toward the street. Holding her under one arm, I ordered an Uber.

"We going to your place?" she asked. "I'll treat you real good, Nick, I promise. You can even fuck my ass."

I helped her shove her arms into her coat as we waited for the car to arrive. As soon as it did, I tucked her inside, then made sure the driver had her address. I had all the dancers' addresses set up on my account for times like this. Stan wouldn't reimburse me, but I didn't give a shit.

"Aren't you coming?" She leaned across the seat toward me.

"Sleep it off," I said. "And clean up those knees or they'll get infected."

I passed a fifty to the driver.

"Already paid," he said in a thick accent. "Your account?" He pointed to his phone.

"I know. Just make sure she gets home, okay? Safe—and alone. If I find out you followed her inside..." I glared at the man.

"Okay, boss. No problem." The driver took the bill, and I closed the door. Angel slumped against the other side, looking about fourteen years old, even though I knew she was a decade older, at least—probably older than me. Shit, this job could be depressing. But at least it was legit.

I headed back into the club. My brothers had scoffed when I'd told them I wanted to go straight. And my da...

I wasn't the one to tell the old man. One of my brothers had ratted me out—most likely Shane—and Da tore a strip off me last time I visited San Quentin. Old man knew the right buttons to push.

Patrick Downey raised us five boys to believe the so-called family business was what we were born to, all we were good for, but he was wrong. At least that's what I kept telling myself, because there was no way I was going to end up spending my life in prison like my old man.

Continue reading... www.maraleigh.com/db1

Made in United States
North Haven, CT
07 January 2025

64083667R00143